Mermaids and

Lions and Other

Mortal Creatures

I0659295

By

Loretta Notto

Mermaids and Lions
And
Other Mortal Creatures

All Rights Reserved

For information address: mickiedaltonbooks@lycos.com

First Published in 2011 in Australia

ISBN: 978-0-9923422-1-0

Published by The Mickie Dalton Foundation
Kempsey, NSW
Australia

www.mickiedaltonfoundation.com

In memory of my parents, Alex and Maria Tedesco, who have given me enough love, life and laughter to fill a book.

Acknowledgements

Thanks to all my friends and family for reading my stories and encouraging me to write more.

Thanks to Ruth, Dusty and the rest of the Amateur Writers Club for reading and critiquing my stories and encouraging me to keep dreaming and writing.

Also many thanks to Brad Van Schaik who took the time to capture my stories beautifully in his artwork.

And a special thanks to Michael Davies, for not only reading my stories and encouraging me to write more, but also for turning those stories into a book for me.

Contents

'T is the Season

Mermaids and Lions and Other Mortal Creatures

Taking Care of Business

The Tower

Jane sits at the mirror and stares into her reflection. She tries to ignore the fine lines quickly forming around her eyes, and instead concentrates on her assets. Naturally blonde with icy blue eyes, she was always able to maintain her bombshell looks. At least until now. She reaches over the counter to pick up the ridiculously long wig. This will probably be her last flick as a 'young maiden.' She's already being considered for a part as a madam in the next movie.

"No thanks to my husband," she mumbles.

"What was that?" Roger sneaks up behind her and lays his hands on her shoulders, making her jump.

"I said, oh, there's my husband," she sputters, and holds up the wig. "Do I really have to wear this thing? I already have long blonde hair."

"Honey, we are producing an adult film featuring Rapunzel. Your own hair is not long enough. You need the extension." Roger sighs and rubs his face. "Maybe you should have stuck to porn flicks. You don't seem to understand much else."

"This isn't much different, is it?" Jane throws down the wig. "Give me a break! I'm doing a bed scene with the Prince, a nude bed scene, for crying out loud!"

"It's an R-rated movie, not an X-rated one. And quit complaining. You're lucky I got you out of that ludicrous business, and into some real movies." Roger's anger softened. "And I married you, didn't I sweetheart? Without prenuptials. That says a lot, doesn't it?"

"Yeah, it says I was too dumb to get a lawyer. Now you control everything."

"Ah, but if anything happens to me, it will all go to you." Roger smirks. "All I ask is that you ignore my, uh, bad habits."

"Oh, you mean your womanizing?" Jane puts on a sweet smile. "Oh sure, I forgive you."

"That's my girl!" Roger gives her a kiss on the cheek.

"As long as your life insurance is paid up," she mumbles.

"What was that?"

"Er, I said too bad those strike talks have been laid up," Jane changes the subject. "How are you going to get the set finished in time for filming with the stage workers on strike?"

"Most of it's done. We just have to get the tower finished. Oh, and we still have to cast a Prince, but that's the easy part." Roger shakes his head. "I'm just having trouble getting people to work on that tower. They don't want to cross the picket line."

"Oh that's not a problem. We'll just get volunteers from the inside." Jane smiles. "As a matter of fact, I found a couple of guys who are willing to help."

Roger gives her a troubled look. "And who would that be?"

"Well, there's Fred from the office, and Glitch from make-up."

Roger stares at her for a moment and then roars with laughter. "You're kidding right? What do they know about building sets? Fred's a computer techie! And Glitch, well, he's just an elf!"

"Don't be ridiculous. Glitch is a make-up artist, and a darn good one at that. He just looks like an elf because, well, he's just really short and had pointy ears and wears a silly green hat." Jane pauses for a moment. "And Fred is an expert on towers."

"Computer towers, Jane, not medieval towers!"

There is a knock on the door. "Hello? It's Fred."

Roger rolls his eyes. "Come in."

Fred and Roger look at each other as they nod their greetings. Where they are similar in height, both a good six feet tall, they differ in looks. Where Roger is paunchy and bald, Fred is athletic with layers of curly brown hair. Except for his wire-rimmed glasses, he does not fit the stereotypical computer geek.

Roger considers this a moment. "Say Fred, can you act? We need a Prince."

Fred chuckles. "I can be a real Prince sometimes. Just ask the ladies in the office." He looks around. "Now, where's the tower that needs repairing?"

Jane smiles at him. "Come along with us, Fred. Glitch is already down there waiting for us."

"Glitch?" Fred shakes his head in confusion as they head out towards the set. "Isn't he that elf in the make-up department?"

A few minutes later, they are out on the set, where Rapunzel's tower sits unfinished. Glitch is sitting by the doorway with a make-up case on his lap. When he sees them, he gets up. "Okay, who needs the manicure?"

Roger looks at him. "I beg your pardon?"

"Jane told me to bring some nails." He holds the case up. "Got 'em right here."

Roger rolls his eyes. "Not those kind of nails! Good grief, I'm in trouble here."

Meanwhile, Fred is looking around. "Um, where's the tower?"

Jane points to the set. Fred raises his eyes a good eighty feet to the top of the tower. He whistles. "Dang biggest computer tower I've ever seen!"

Roger starts to chuckle. Soon it turns into an uncontrollable laugh. After a few moments, he catches his breath. "Okay, fellas, the top floor window has to be installed with a fake braid that will be thrown out for the Prince to climb." He takes Jane by the arm. "My wife and I are going out for lunch. Have fun." He starts to laugh again as he leads Jane away

Two hours later, Roger and Jane come back to find Fred and Glitch sitting on a picnic table eating sandwiches.

"Well," Roger smirks. "How goes the hair-raising adventure?"

Fred gulps down the last of his lunch and smiles. "All done boss. Hair is installed."

Glitch looks up at Roger's shiny forehead. "You know, we could do the same for you."

"Don't get smart!" Roger scowls. "Show me what you've done."

"Stay right there, boss," Fred says. "C'mon Glitch, let's go up the tower and show him what we've done."

"Oh, let me come too!" Jane says and follows them up the spiral stairway inside the tower.

Moments later, Roger sees a large braid of golden hair tumble out of the top floor window and down the side of the tower. Fred sticks his head out the window. "There you go, boss. Now all we need is a Prince!"

Roger walks up to the braid and runs his hand over it. He gives it a good yank. Unable to resist, he slips his foot into the braid, where there is a rope ladder built in for easy climbing. He starts to climb up.

Jane looks out the window and sees her husband climbing. "What are you doing?" she yells. "It hasn't been tested yet!"

"I'm testing it now!" he yells back.

Jane, Fred and Glitch watch as Roger slowly makes his way up the braid. Just as he nears the top, there is a loud groaning sound. Suddenly, the braid pulls away from the wall, and falls to the foot of the tower, along with the screeching Roger. Jane lets out a scream and looks down to find her husband's grotesquely twisted body lying motionless on the ground.

For a moment, all three stare down at the scene. Then they all start laughing.

"It worked! It really worked!" Fred says. "Jane, you're a genius!" He plants a passionate kiss on her mouth. "All that money he has... and it's ours!"

"I just hope we can pull this off," Glitch looks worried. "One-third of his dough isn't going to help any of us if we end up in jail."

"You know Glitch, you're right." Fred considers this for a moment. "I know, we need to make it look like we tried to help him." He quickly pushes Glitch out the window. Moments later, his lifeless body is at the bottom of the tower next to Roger's.

"Aw, poor Glitch... what a hero, trying to save Roger from falling." Fred looks at Jane and fakes a sad look. "And now we just have to split the dough in half. Once we get to Mexico, of course."

Jane puts her arms around Fred. "Oh my Prince, you know I'd go anywhere with you." She leans over to kiss him, but instead gives him a push out the window. She watches him fall and sighs. "Too bad you had to be a hero too!"

She studies the scene below for a moment. Satisfied with what she sees, she begins to scream at the top of her lungs. "Help, somebody help! There's been a terrible accident!"

Dinner for Two

It's been a gruelling day at the office and Sally is more than happy to see five o'clock finally arrive. She shuts down her computer and puts her filing aside for another day. On her way out, she pokes her head into her co-worker's office.

"I'm heading out, Dan," she tells him. "I was planning to try that new Chinese restaurant down the street before going home. Care to join me?"

"Oh, you mean Dinner for Two?"

Sally chuckles. "Well, I guess it would be if we went together. Although it sounds a little too cosy. I don't think your wife would like that."

"No, no, I meant the name of the restaurant," Dan says.

"Oh, I'm afraid I don't know the name of the restaurant," Sally knits her brows together pensively.

"That is the name of the restaurant!"

"What is?"

"Dinner for Two!" Dan sighs. Sally is a good worker, but sometimes she can be a little daft. "Okay, I'll grab a bite with you. Dawn isn't coming home till late anyway."

"Oh good," Sally says. "Dinner for two it is! Say, you wouldn't happen to know the name of that restaurant, would you?"

Later on, Sally and Dan are seated at a small but comfortable table, looking the menu over.

"Oh look!" Sally exclaims. She points to the front of the menu. "The name of this place is Dinner for Two!"

Dan sighs. "So it is. So, what are you going to have?"

"Well, since we both like the same Chinese food, why don't we order their dinner for two?"

Dan peruses the menu. "I don't think they have a dinner for two, Sally. I guess this isn't your stereotypical Chinese restaurant."

"Why, that's crazy! Why would they call this place Dinner for Two if they don't have a dinner for two?"

"It's just a popular phrase for a Chinese restaurant, I guess."

Just then, the waiter approaches their table. "May I take your order?"

Sally looks him over. "You're not Chinese," she says.

"No madam, I'm quite Caucasian," he replies.

"Well, first there is no dinner for two in a restaurant called Dinner for Two, then we don't even have a waiter of Asian origin serving us." Sally shakes her head. "What kind of Chinese restaurant is this?"

Dan and the waiter reply at the same time. "Not your stereotypical one!"

The waiter continues. "Look, if it makes it easier, you can give me your order and I can multiply it by two. Voila... dinner for two."

"Voila?" Sally looks confused. "Isn't that French?"

"Sorry, I don't know the phrase in Chinese."

"Well, of course you wouldn't, silly!" Sally giggles. "You're not Chinese!"

Dan runs his fingers nervously through his hair. "Look, why don't you just surprise us with a dinner for two," he tells the exasperated waiter.

"Good idea," the waiter replies, and returns to the kitchen.

They relax over a couple of glasses of wine while waiting for their dinner. Sally giggles again. "Gee, he must have a heck of a time explaining this Dinner for Two thing to his patrons."

Dan pats her shoulder. "I'm sure he does, Sally." He chuckles. "I'm sure he does."

A Lesson for Mr. Higgins

October 26, 1968

Mr. Higgins silently entered the classroom. He noticed the quiet buzz, typical for a group of 12-year-olds who have been left without a teacher for several minutes. Some of the students noticed his entrance and quickly stood up. The more studious ones had their heads buried in their books and did not stand at his entrance. Unfortunately, they would be the ones to get reprimanded.

"What did I tell you about standing whenever a teacher enters the room!" he hollered at the class, startling those still sitting. They quickly stood up, but it was too late. "I want all the students who were sitting to stay after school for detention!"

"But Sir..." Tommy bravely challenged him.

"No buts, and you will stay longer for that!"

Lorrie quietly sighed. She admired Tommy's courage, but he wasn't very smart. Nobody challenges Mr. Higgins.

"Do you have a problem, Lorrie?" Mr. Higgins directed his sharp gaze towards her.

"Sir?" Lorrie paled. She stood up and felt herself shaking.

"I heard you sigh. Do you have a problem?"

"No Sir."

"Good. Then you can keep Tommy company during his longer detention."

"Yes Sir."

Later that afternoon, twenty minutes after the others left, Mr. Higgins excused Tommy and Lorrie. The two students walked along the route they shared to their homes. Both were loaded down with books as, like every evening, they faced hours of homework. Lorrie recalled several nights where she'd worked from the moment she got home until well into the night, with only a couple of hours' sleep. She could see Tommy struggling to keep a grip on his books. His hands were still welted and hurting from getting the strap the day before.

"Man, I hate this teacher," he mumbled. "We've only had him for two months. I can't take a whole year of this! I've been given the strap before, but none of the other teachers ever left marks on my hands like this."

"And if he isn't hurting somebody physically, he's hurting somebody's feelings!" Lorrie sighed. "He's always embarrassing me about something."

Tommy was silent a moment, and then he giggled. "Heh, maybe we should get that old witch on McElroy Street to cast a spell on him. Turn him into a toad, or something."

Lorrie stopped in her tracks. "Tommy, that's a great idea!"

"Huh?"

"Maybe she can help us!"

Tommy gulped. "Uh, I was just kidding, Lorrie... I don't think we should be bothering a witch, especially this time of year."

"This is the best time to bother her. She decorates her house up for Halloween and gives out great treats every year. She'll be in a great mood to help us kids!"

"Well, you go ahead and ask her then." They reached Tommy's street. "I gotta go. See you tomorrow." He quickly walked towards his house.

Lorrie watched him go, and sighed. So much for the courageous classroom brat, she thought to herself. She slowly walked home, but came to a stop when she reached McElroy Street. She looked towards the witch's house. She could see the witch on her front lawn, setting up Halloween decorations. Without a second thought, Lorrie hurried towards her.

Rachel Leary was putting the finishing touches on a scarecrow when she felt a pair of eyes on her. She turned around to see a familiar young girl staring at her with a terrified look. She smiled at her.

"Hi there. You're the Torelli girl, aren't you?"

"Y-yes," Lorrie stuttered. "H-how are you today, Miss Leary?"

"Oh just fine, thank you!" Rachel looked around. "It's a lovely time of year, don't you think?" She looked back at Lorrie. "That's quite a load of books you have there. Listen, I just made some fresh pumpkin cookies. Would you like some?"

Lorrie studied the witch. She had long, dark, wildly curly hair and was dressed in black pants and a black sweater. She would have looked like the perfect witch if it weren't for her eyes. They were the warmest brown eyes Lorrie had ever seen. They sent a wave of comfort to her, and she found herself accepting the offer of cookies.

Minutes later, they were sitting in Rachel's kitchen and talking about Lorrie's teacher. "I don't know what to do," Lorrie explained. "He's such a tough teacher. See these books? Homework in every subject, every night. Sometimes he makes us stay after school for hours to do extra work. And he always embarrasses me when I don't know the answer to something."

"Oh my," Rachel gave her a sympathetic look. Suddenly, Lorrie started to cry. Rachel came around the table and gave the young girl a hug. "There, there now. Isn't there anything your parents can do?"

Lorrie sniffed. "My parents met him on parent-teacher night. They like him and don't seem to understand what I'm upset about." She looked up at Rachel. "Miss Leary, could you cast a spell on him? Maybe just wiggle your nose and turn him into a gorilla or something?"

Rachel burst out laughing. "My dear, you've been watching too much television. I can't turn anybody into anything. I can't even turn him into a nice guy!" She looked thoughtful for a moment. She looked at Lorrie. "But I am pretty good with dreams." She got up and started to clear the plates and glasses away. "Why don't you head on home. I guarantee you by this time tomorrow your Mr. Higgins will have learned a big lesson in life."

Lorrie thanked Rachel for the cookies. She may not have gotten Mr. Higgins turned into an animal, but at least she felt better talking about it. As she headed down the street, she thought she heard Rachel's voice whispering...

Oh kindly spirits, a dream I would seek,

For the school master who feeds on the meek,

Give him the future for him to see,

And teach him a lesson, so mote it be...

December 25, 1968

John Higgins woke up with a bad headache. He looked around his small bachelor apartment and blinked. Everything felt surreal, as if he was in a dream. He made some coffee and sat down to some breakfast. As he

13

munched some toast, he thought about his students. Not a bad bunch of kids, but they still need to learn respect. That Tommy is going to be trouble this year, he can see that. And the Torelli girl... well, she is so shy, and such a gangly kid. He hated picking on her, but it was for her own good. She's going to have to learn how to be tough in this world...

An hour later, he entered the classroom. And froze. The class did not stand up for him, but he didn't notice that. There was something wrong with each of the students. They all looked horribly pale, and they seemed transparent. He swore he could see right through each child.

"What the..." He shook his head again and slowly sat down at his desk. His headache never ceased. The students all smiled eerie smiles at him.

"Got a problem, Sir?" Tommy asked him.

"W-what is going on?" Mr. Higgins answered weakly.

"Don't you remember, Sir?" said another student.

"Come on, Sir, you're the reason we're all dead!" yelled another.

Mr. Higgins gasped. "We're dead?"

"You're not dead," said Tommy. "We are!" He went on to explain. "Yesterday was Christmas Eve. We were all excited about finishing school early, so we got a little noisy. When the rest of the school was dismissed at noon, you kept us here for the afternoon. You then left us here to do homework while you went to the teacher's lounge on the other side of the school. When you came back, it was too late."

Mr. Higgins rubbed his face. "I still don't understand how you died."

"Carbon monoxide poisoning! The classroom is right above the furnace room." Tommy smiled his eerie smile. The students all got up and surrounded Mr. Higgins. Tommy continued. "We decided that since you loved keeping us here after school so much, we would give you a nice Christmas present. We are going to keep you here, undead, with us forever. Merry Christmas, Sir!"

Tommy started laughing, along with the rest of the students. The laughter was hollow and it crept right through Mr. Higgins, making his hair stand on end. He began to panic and scream. The students continued to laugh. He continued to scream...

October 27, 1968

Mr. Higgins entered the classroom, his head heavy from a restless night and a horrific nightmare. The students dutifully stood up.

"Class, please sit," he quietly told them. He forced himself to look at them and felt a wave of relief to see they were quite alive. He took a deep breath and started to speak.

"I realize that I'm a tough teacher. I take pride in my profession, therefore I like to use strong tactics to mould a class into something I can be proud of." He paused for a moment. "Unfortunately, I have been forgetting that in order to earn respect, I must give respect. And for that I apologize."

He picked up a math text. "Now, let's get down to business. Tommy, can you give us the answer to the first question?"

Mr. Higgins looked at Tommy. Tommy smiled his eerie smile...

The Land of the Free

"That'll be $3.79 altogether, please." I smiled dutifully at the customer.

The woman frowned. "That sounds like too much, even with tax. The sign said $1.99."

"Let me check." I trotted over to where she picked up the throat drops, and spotted the expired sale sign that was overlooked when the sale was taken off. I came back to the check out. "You're right, ma'am. Sorry for the trouble. I will adjust the price accordingly."

"Don't I get it for free?"

I started to chuckle at the joke that all of our customers seemed to use. But one look at her told me she was serious. "I beg your pardon?"

"When the price rings up wrong, the customer is supposed to get the product for free. It's the law."

I blinked. "Ma'am, I realize that a lot of the larger franchises offer that courtesy, but we are a small, independent business. We simply offer the price that the customer was misled to believe. I know we live in the Land of the Free, but I think the "free" offer is just a courtesy. I don't think it's the law. If it is, then nobody has been told about it."

"Well, it is the law. I suggest you look it up."

"Ma'am, if I am breaking the law, then I suggest you call the police. If not, that'll be $2.29 for the throat drops."

The customer paid and smiled sweetly at me. "Look it up." Then she left.

I put my head on the counter. I could hear John snickering. "Having a bad day, are you?"

I looked up. "One of many. I need a break."

He laughed. "What you need is a couple of weeks at a retreat or something."

"Hah, not with what you pay me!"

John pretended to be flabbergasted. "Is that any way to talk to your boss?"

I chuckled. "I meant what I said, though... about the break. I could use one."

"Sure, no problem. I'll send Janie out to take over. Then you can go on your fifteen minute Retreat of Golden Silence in the back room." He started to head to the back of the store, then turned around. "Oh and don't forget to indulge in one of our mindless activities while you are there. May I suggest the thumb-twiddling? You're good at that!" With a hearty laugh, he continued to the back of the store.

A few minutes later, I was lying down on the couch in our staff room, clearing my mind and hoping to relax. I did even better than relax. I fell asleep.

I found myself flying, arms out like an airplane, through the clear blue sky. I soared over farmland, mountains and oceans, and within minutes I was soaring towards some beautiful islands. I crash-landed painlessly (after all, this was a dream) in front of what looked like a pretty Hawaiian hotel. Just outside the door, there was a sign that read, "$50 per night".

I entered the lobby and approached the front desk.

"I would like to stay for one night, please," I said to the smiling hotel clerk.

"Certainly. That'll be $79 please."

I looked at the clerk. "I believe your sign said $50."

"Let me check." She disappeared for a few moments, and then came back. "You're right, Ma'am. Sorry for the trouble. The rates just went up, and we forgot to change the sign. I will adjust your price accordingly."

"Don't I get it for free?" I found myself saying.

The clerk blinked. "I beg your pardon?"

"This is the Land of the Free, so I am supposed to get the room for free if the price rings up wrong."

"In your dreams!" The clerk started to laugh.

"That's right, this is my dream, so I should get it for free. Why, I'll call the police on you!"

"Who are you going to call, the Dream Team?"

She continued to laugh. Feeling more battered and torn than a disrespected American flag, I went back outside. I decided fly back to work, so I began to flap my arms.

Moments later, I felt someone shaking me. I could hear John's voice. "Wake up, will you? And why are you flapping your arms?"

I opened my eyes, and got up off the couch. "Guess I'd better get back to work."

John nodded. "Good idea. Oh, and can you put the cough drops on sale? Make it a "Buy 1 Get 1 Free" special."

I looked at him and shook my head. "John, this may be the Land of the Free, but nothing in life is free." And with that, I went back to work.

Closed Door

Sally rushed into the house and through the hallway into the kitchen, where Kevin had already started supper.

"Oh, there you are," Kevin turned away from the stove for a moment. "I guess that detour you have to take really gets backed up during rush hour."

Sally kissed his cheek. "Oh no, it wasn't that. I took a detour of my own." She sighed and shook her head. "A very strange one."

Kevin looked at her. "What happened?"

"Oh nothing serious." She began cutting some tomatoes for the salad. "Remember that advertisement for a retirement home complex up north that sounded really nice? Well, I noticed a sign for it on one of the buildings on the detour route. So I thought I'd stop by it and maybe get some information for us."

Kevin knitted his brows. "I didn't realize they've set up an office here in town."

"Yes, they did. The sign said, "Closed Door – We help you finalize your final home.""

Kevin's eyes widened. Then he smiled. "So you went in?"

"Yes." Sally shook her head. "It was strange, so strange..."

Sally had entered the charming little house that was now used as the Closed Door facility. She caught a whiff of carnations in the air and it sent an odd shiver down her spine. The scent was soon forgotten as a young man dressed in a sombre dark suit approached her.

"Hello, I'm John McKenzie. May I help you?"

Sally shook his hand. "Hello Mr. McKenzie, I'm Sally Monty. I would like some information on your retirement homes."

Mr. McKenzie chuckled. "Well, that is a charming way of putting it. Please come into my office."

They entered a simple but pleasant office, and sat down.

Sally began. "I guess I would have to start by buying a lot."

"Oh, you mean, a plot."

"Oh, I thought it was called a lot. How big are they? We don't want anything too big. We may not be in the greatest condition to be mowing the lawn by then."

Mr. McKenzie smiled. "I should say not. But we do have the lawn mowed for our patrons. We even care for your stones."

Sally looked confused. "My stones?"

"Oh, forgive me. Perhaps you wish to be cremated?"

"Please Mr. McKenzie, one step at a time! I want to buy a home first."

"But you will need to know if you prefer burial or cremation before you make your plans. How else will you know what size, er, home you would like?"

Sally shook her head. "This is so confusing. Both my husband and I wish to be buried, but not in our retirement home."

Mr. McKenzie sighed. "You're right, Mrs. Monty, this is very confusing." He opened his desk drawer and pulled out a large envelope. "Why don't I just give you our basic information package? You can look it over with your husband and then you can decide what kind of final resting place you would like."

Sally took the package. "Thank you. Oh my, I never realized how difficult the last years of my life can be." She left the office.

Now, she stopped cutting tomatoes and picked up the package she had brought in. She handed it to Kevin. He looked at it and burst out laughing.

"What's so funny?" Sally asked.

Still chuckling, Kevin picked up another package that was on the table and handed it to her. "I called that 1-800 number for an information package on that retirement home complex. I just got it today."

Sally looked down at the package and began to laugh too. "Guess I got things a little mixed up." She read the logo on the package out loud. "Opened Door – We help you finalize the beginning of the rest of your life."

Have Your Cake

"Have Your Cake, can I help you?"

"Joey, is that you?"

Joey felt the familiar chill travel down his spine whenever he heard Dante's voice. "Yeah, it's me."

"Okay, listen up," Dante's raspy voice pierced Joey's ear. "You'll be getting the package this morning. You know what to do with it. Don't mess up." The line went dead.

Joey sighed. Two years ago, he had asked Dante for a sizable loan so that he could set up his pastry business, Have Your Cake. Dante was more than happy to help out. Now Joey was not only paying back the money, but he was also returning the favour. Many times over.

He went back to the birthday cake he was decorating. It was a large, square cake, at least six inches deep. Deep enough to bury the contents of Dante's said package, he thought. He shook his head. You couldn't settle for a lifetime supply of free pastry, could you, Dante? He checked his watch. 5:00 a.m. He hoped the package got there before his two employees did.

Two hours and one delivered package later, Joey was putting the final touches on the cake's icing when the phone rang.

"Joey, is that you?"

This time he felt the familiar tug at his heart whenever he heard his old girlfriend's voice. "Hi Trisha."

"How's my wedding cake coming along?"

"I'll have it ready for you today." He held back a sigh.

"Oh, thank you so much!" Trisha cooed. "I know I don't need it until Saturday, but there's plenty of room in our fridge, so could you have it delivered today?"

"Sure, Trisha, will do."

Trisha was silent for a moment. "Joey, thank you for helping me out. I hope it wasn't too awkward, what with us having a history together. But you make the best cakes in town..."

"Not a problem, Trisha," he said with an upbeat he didn't feel. "I wish you both the best."

"Thank you, Joey."

As he hung up the phone, his two employees came in. "Morning," Sandra and Rob said in unison. They stopped in their tracks.

"Whoa Joey, are you okay?" Sandra asked him. "You look a little pale."

Joey rubbed his eyes. "I'm a little tired. Look, can you guys finish up the two orders for me? The Pops birthday cake just needs to be decorated, as does the Feeney wedding cake." He took off his apron. "I'm going to lie down in the back for a bit. Rob, you can deliver the wedding cake today, and the customer will be picking up the birthday cake here later."

"Sure thing, Joey!" Rob and Sandra began their tasks as Joey went to his office. He lay down on the couch and fell asleep.

Joey woke up with a start. He looked at his watch. 2:00 p.m.! He jumped up and hurried to the front shop. Sandra and Rob were cleaning up the kitchen area.

"Joey! You look much better," Sandra remarked. "And everything is going smoothly. We took care of the lunch crowd, both orders are done and Rob has already delivered the Feeney wedding cake."

"Oh good," Joey nodded and looked around. He stopped and stared at the round, two-tier cake and felt his stomach twist into a knot. "Um, why does the wedding cake have "Happy Birthday Pops" written on it? And where is the square cake?" But he already knew the answer.

Rob gasped and Sandra blanched. "Oh oh..." They said in unison.

Joey stared at them for a moment. Then he ran out of the shop and into the parking lot. He quickly got into his car and tore out of the lot.

"Damn damn damn!" he muttered as he drove to Trisha's house. "You guys never make those kinds of mistakes," he berated his employees, although he was alone in the car. "Why now?"

Ten minutes later, he pulled into Trisha's driveway. He got out of the car, ran to her door and rang the doorbell. "Okay," he mumbled as he waited. "This can still be salvaged..." Trisha's mother opened the door.

"Joey!" She exclaimed. "Hello dear, how have you been?"

"Fine thanks, Mrs. Feeney, but I need the cake back right away!"

"Oh, er..." Momentarily startled, Mrs. Feeney said, "The cake isn't here."

"Huh?"

"Now dear, you shouldn't say 'huh'. You're a business man, and your grammar should be a little better than that," Mrs. Feeney gently admonished while patting him on the cheek.

Joey took a deep breath and calmly took her hand into his two. "Mrs. Feeney, please help me. The wrong cake was delivered here, and I need it back right away."

"I wish I could help you, dear, but I don't know where it is. Both the cake and Trisha disappeared." She patted his two hands with her free one. "When you find her, could you talk her out of getting married to that jerk? I'd really like to see her back with you. You're such a sweetheart." She took her hands away from his. "Now I must get back inside. I still have a lot of preparations to take care of for this ridiculous wedding." She turned around and went back into the house."

"But Mrs Feeney..." The door slammed shut in his face. "Dear sweet scatterbrained woman," he mumbled and went back to his car.

He stayed in the driveway for a few minutes, thinking. He'd successfully placed the package into Dante's birthday cake. He didn't know what was in the small white bag or what Dante was going to do with it, but judging by the weight of it, he'd bet it was cocaine. And if it was cocaine, his ex-girlfriend was running around somewhere with a cake full of drugs. He picked up his cell phone and regretted not keeping Trisha's number. He was about to call the shop and was startled when the cell phone rang in his hand. It showed the shop's number.

"Rob?" he answered.

"Hey Joey," Rob said, "Trisha Feeney brought the wedding cake back."

Joey breathed a sigh of relief. "Thank God. Is she still there?"

"Yeah, but so is Mr. Dante. And he doesn't look too happy."

"Oh great," Joey muttered. "Tell them both I'm on my way back."

Ten minutes later, he parked his car in the lot and worked his way to the shop, all the time muttering, "I'm dead, I'm dead, I'm dead..."

When he stepped into the shop, he was surprised to see Dante and Tricia sitting at a table, eating pastries and drinking coffee.

"Joey!" Tricia jumped up and gave him a hug. "I was just telling Mr Dante about how we used to go out, but now I'm marrying somebody else and you're still sweet enough to make my wedding cake." She took a breath. "Except it's not really my cake, is it? It's Mr Dante's birthday cake in disguise!" She giggled.

Joey looked at Dante, expecting to see one furious mobster, but he was actually smiling. Relief washed over him and he silently thanked Tricia for using her unending charm to pacify him.

"Yeah, I'm sorry about that." Joey said. "We'll take care of it right away."

Tricia looked over to the far table where the two cakes sat side by side with Sandra and Rob hovering over them, "You know, that square cake is so pretty, I wouldn't mind keeping it as my wedding cake, and Joey can make another one for Mr Dante."

"NO!" Both Dante and Joey yelled in unison. Trisha, Sandra and Rob all jumped. Dante cleared his throat. "What I mean is, my Pops is superstitious so it has to be the original cake."

"Ah, look Trisha, can we talk for a minute?" Joey took Trisha's hand and proceeded to lead her to his office. Dante stepped in front of him.

"Where do you think you're going?" he said to Joey. "You still owe me a birthday cake."

27

Joey sighed. He turned to Sandra and Rob and wagged a finger at the cakes. "Fix this, will you?" He turned back towards his office, but Dante was still standing in the way.

"Um, this is kind of private," Joey said.

"That's okay; I'm a private kind of guy." Dante retorted. "You can talk right here."

"Okay, fine!" Joey turned to Trisha. "You can't get married on Saturday."

Trisha looked confused. "Why not?"

"B-because," Joey stuttered. "Because... your mother thinks that I'm the one you should be marrying!" He cleared his throat. "And so do I."

Trisha stared at him. "Well." She let out a deep breath. "Well. Funny you should mention that. Mr Dante and I were talking about the same thing."

Joey looked at Dante, then back at Trisha. "I beg your pardon?"

Dante put his arm around Joey's shoulder, best-buddy style. "Yeah, you see, I know the jerk she's marrying, and he's no good for a nice lady like her. Now you," He poked Joey in the shoulder. "You are a good guy. Fine business man, nice looking. Not that I notice fellas in that manner," he quickly added. "So then I find out that Trisha doesn't even love this guy. Said if she couldn't be with you, it didn't matter who she ended up with." He snorted. "Go figure." He let go of Joey.

Joey looked at Trisha. "Is that true?"

Trisha smiled and poked Joey in the shoulder, mimicking Dante. "Yeah, it's true." She put her arms around him and kissed him.

"Well, my work is done here." Dante walked towards the redecorated and now boxed birthday cake, "I'll just grab my cake and go." He picked it up and turned towards Joey and Trisha, who were now arm in arm and watching him. "Oh, and as your wedding gift, your debt is paid. No more money owing, and no more favours owing."

"Well, thanks Dante!" Joey walked towards him and shook his hand.

"Not a problem," Dante held up his cake. "I figured after this fiasco, you might end up as a liability anyway."

"What can I say?" Joey offered. "You can't have your cake and eat it too."

Dante rolled his eyes. "That is so corny." He walked out of the shop, smiling at the chorus of laughter behind him.

The Firefighter's Nightmares

The little girl is curled up on her bed, hands over her ears, her favourite dolly tucked close to her tummy. Where's Mommy? Why isn't she coming to get her? Uncle Frank once told her what to do if that smoky alarm thing ever rang, but now she can't remember what it was... She sees smoke coming through the bottom of her door... Oh, now she remembers... She takes her blanky off the bed and pushes it against the bottom of the door... there, that's better... Where's Mommy? Maybe she's being a 'coholic. Uncle Frank doesn't visit any more because he doesn't like the way Mommy drinks that funny stuff and sleeps so much, and that she is a 'coholic. The little girl misses Uncle Frank and wishes that he could be there right now so that he could tell her what to do... MOMMY!!! ...

MOMMY!!! The child's scream brought Amanda back to the present. As did the shout from her platoon captain, Eric.

"You gonna get moving, Saunders, or you gonna let that little boy fry?"

"Moving, sir!" She began the difficult climb up the aerial ladder to the fourth floor of the burning building.

Amanda was the only woman in the city's fire department. She worked hard to build her strength and her knowledge, since the department did not lower its standards for female applicants. As it should be, she always thought. People's lives depended on firefighters getting them out danger, and doing it quickly. But she would never admit that hauling all that equipment plus a body or two up and down sixty feet of ladder was much tougher for her than it was for her male counterparts.

Not that the guys would harass her about it. She had their respect. Not only was she "Frank's Girl", but she was also a damn good firefighter.

Now if she could only learn to leave the past in the past.

When she reached the open fourth floor window, she noticed smoke was beginning to come through it. Not a good sign. She quickly pushed in the screen and squeezed herself into the small room. She could hear whimpering, and was relieved to know the child stayed in the room. She quickly worked her way through the haze and closed the bedroom door, cutting off the smoke. Even though it was a sunny day, she still had to use her flashlight to find the little boy. She saw him on the bed, where she knew he would be.

"Hey little guy, are you okay?"

"Mommy!" The little boy began to cough from the smoke. He looked at her and cowered.

"It's okay... I'm a firefighter and I'm here to help you. This is just all the stuff we have to wear. So don't be afraid, okay?"

The little boy nodded and coughed some more. Amanda judged him to be about six or seven. And where was his mother, out on a binge? She felt a flush of anger, but quickly suppressed it.

"Now, I'm going to pick you up and pass you to another firefighter. He'll bring you down the ladder. Just hang on to him, and you'll be okay."

The little boy nodded again. She lifted the small boy and easily passed him to Eric, who had come up the ladder behind her to wait just outside the window.

"Good job Saunders!" he said to her as he positioned the boy over his shoulder. "Hurry on and come back out this way. There's no one left in the building."

He then spoke to the little boy. "And your mommy is safe. Ready to go see her? Hang on!" And with that, he began the descent down the ladder....

"Hang on!" The little girl hears a familiar voice outside her window. "Amanda, you in there? Hang on!"

"Uncle Frank!" She runs to the open window and presses her face to the screen. She can see a bunch of fire trucks and lots of firemen running around. She knows all about fire and the fire 'partment because Uncle Frank is a fireman. "Uncle Frank, help!"

"Stay right there, Amanda, I'm coming!" She can see the ladder coming towards her window. Her fear disappears. Uncle Frank will save her, and she will even get to go down the ladder with him. She is smiling now. She's just decided she is going to be a fireman when she grows up...

"Saunders, what are you doing? Get your ass down here!" Eric's shout once again brought Amanda to the present. She climbed over the windowsill and onto the ladder. On the climb down, she noticed that most of the apartment building was engulfed in flames. She was amazed that no one got hurt. And hopefully it would stay that way as they finished battling the flames.

When she reached ground level, she could see the reunion and the happy faces of both mother and child. She felt a hand on her shoulder.

"You did good, Saunders," Eric told her. He stared at her for a moment. "It brought back the memory, didn't it, Amanda?" Uncle Frank had trained Eric when he first joined the fire department. He had become a good friend of his, and in turn had trained Amanda when she joined the department. He knew about her past and about her nightmares...

Uncle Frank carries Amanda down the ladder, and away from the fire. "You're going to be okay now, sweetie. You did good up there. You remembered to close the door and seal the bottom!"

Amanda smiles at him. "When I grow up I'm going to be a fireman just like you!"

Uncle Frank laughs. "And you'll be a good one too!"

Amanda looks around. "Where's Mommy?"

Uncle Frank's smile disappears. "We're not sure yet, honey. Do you remember where she was before you went to bed?"

"She was sitting by the fireplace." Amanda pouts. "She was drinking that yucky stuff again."

"She never did get that fireplace fixed, did she," Uncle Frank says this more to himself than to her.

Suddenly Amanda is afraid again. She hugs Uncle Frank. "Please don't ever leave me again, please!"

Uncle Frank hugs her back. "I won't sweetie. No matter what happens, I won't."...

The hand on her shoulder tightened. Amanda shook off the past again and looked at Eric.

"Amanda, you just saved a little boy's life. You gave that mother her child, safe and sound." Eric smiled. "I know you weren't that lucky. You were about the same age as him when your mother died in that fire. But then again, you were lucky enough to have Frank adopt you. I'd say both the tragedy and the luck made you a fine firefighter, and a fine person."

Eric and Amanda stood for a few moments and watched as the last of the fire was put out.

Eric turned back to her. "Time to put those nightmares back into the past where they belong."

Amanda nodded. "You're right. I have a future full of saving lives. I don't have time for the past any more. From now on, no more nightmares!"

Eric chuckled. "Well, not about fires, anyway. I can't guarantee you won't have other ones."

Amanda laughed. "Well, it'll be a nice change of scenery, anyway!"

That night, for the first time in her life, Amanda felt a sense of peace. She closed her eyes and hoped for a different dream...

"Mommy, is that you?" Amanda is standing in the burnt rubble of the fire she and her platoon had fought that day. Her mother is standing in front of her.

"Yes Amanda, it's me." Mommy is looking her up and down. Amanda realizes that she is wearing her firefighting gear. Mommy continues to speak. "Look at you, all grown up and a firefighter. I'm so proud of you."

Amanda feels anger burning her face. "No thanks to you!" she yells at her mother.

Mommy nods. "I understand your anger. I was an alcoholic, and because of it, I died. And I almost killed you." She moves her hands towards Amanda, but doesn't touch her. "But look at how things turned out. If I didn't die, Frank would never have adopted you. You may never have become a firefighter. And even if you did, you may not have been there today to save that little boy's life."

Amanda feels the anger fading. "That's what I always tell myself. Things always happen for a reason."

"I'm sorry, Amanda."

Amanda smiles. "Mommy, I think I've forgiven you a long time ago."

Mommy smiles back. "I'm glad. Good-bye Amanda." She disappears...

Amanda woke up from her dream. She smiled at the fact that it was indeed a dream. Her nightmares were over.

The Little Perverts

The two boys stood in front of the Burly Esquire. Two large, red doors stood surrounded by glassed-in pictures of women in various stages of undress.

Dorian stared at the neon sign above the door. "What does 'Burly Esquire' mean?"

"Huh?" Matt tore his eyes away from the pictures. "Oh, um, I dunno. My brother Greg says they got it from the word 'burlesque'."

"What does 'burlesque' mean?"

Matt shrugged his shoulders. "Dunno that either. But Greg says this is where women take off their clothes."

Dorian scratched his head. "Why?"

Matt stared at the pictures again. "I think 'cause men like looking at boobs."

Dorian's eyes widened. "I'm not allowed to say 'boobs'. My mom says she'll wash out my mouth with soap if I do. I'm s'posed to call 'em 'breasts'."

"I said 'boobs' once, and my mom just laughed and called me a pervert."

"What's a pervert?"

Matt shrugged his shoulders again. "I dunno."

"Well, hello little blossoms!" The two boys jumped at the deep female voice. They both turned around to find a willowy blonde in a tight mini-dress and knee high leather boots. "What are you fellas up to?"

Dorian gulped. "Nothing, Ma'am. We were, um, just looking, um..."

The blonde laughed. "That's what they all say!" She bent over to bring her head closer to the boys. Matt gawked at the ample amount of flesh falling out of her neckline.

"How would you boys like to come in and take a look around?"

The two boys looked at each other. Dorian whispered to Matt. "Should we? She's a stranger."

Matt whispered back. "Yeah, but it's not like we're getting into a car with a man or anything. We can both beat her up if we have to."

The blonde laughed. "Don't worry fellas, I'm not a pervert."

Matt smiled. "I am!" he said proudly.

The blonde laughed again. "Come on in, fellas! By the way, my name is Windy." She opened the door.

"I'm Matt."

"I'm Dorian, but my mom calls me Windy after I eat beans." Dorian looked at Windy. "Is that why they call you Windy too?"

Windy smiled. "No hun, in my profession, it's not a good idea to eat beans." She shooed the boys through the door in front of her and let it close behind them.

Once their eyes adjusted to the dim lighting, they could see the red and black décor of the lounge. A small catwalk ran down the middle of the room, with a pole at each end.

"What are those poles for?" Dorian asked Windy.

"It's part of our, ah, dance act," she answered.

Matt looked around the empty room. "How come nobody's here?"

"It's too early yet. We girls come here in the afternoon to practice our dancing."

"Can we watch?" both boys said at the same time.

"No you may not!" Another female voice bellowed across the room, once again making the boys jump. An older, gray-haired woman walked towards them, flashing

Windy a look of disdain. "What were you thinking letting these young boys in here?"

"Aw Kathy, I was just having a little fun!"

"First of all, I can see several laws that have just been broken, not to mention the moral wrongs!"

Windy giggled. "Kathy, you're a grandmother, yet you own a strip joint! You wanna talk about morals?"

Kathy sighed. "Go get changed for practice. And don't come out until I've got these boys out of here!"

Windy smiled and waved at the boys. "Bye fellas!"

"Bye Windy!" The boys waved back.

When Windy left the lounge, Kathy turned back to the boys.

"Are we in trouble?" Matt asked.

"No, of course not," Kathy answered. "It's just that this is not a nice place for children to be."

"My big brother Greg comes here all the time!" Matt covered his mouth. "I'm not really supposed to know that, but Greg says I'll understand some day."

Kathy sighed. "Yes, I'm sure you will."

Matt bravely rambled on. "I like looking at boobs..." Dorian elbowed him. "I mean, breasts. Sometimes I sneak into Greg's room and look at his magazines! And I kissed Melissa, she's a girl in my class, but she said she didn't like it..." His voice trailed away.

Kathy smiled. "How old are you, Son?"

"I'm ten. So is Dorian."

"Well, you boys will be young men before you know it. And like your brother said, you will understand some day. All I can hope for is that you learn to respect women."

Dorian's face brightened. "That's what my mom says!"

Kathy nodded. "Well, your mom is right. Now, you'd best get out of here before the law throws the book at me." She went over to the bar and reached into a small glass plate. "Here's a couple of loonies each. Go on down to the ice cream shop and have a treat. It's on the house."

"Thank you, ma'am!" The two boys took the coins and headed out the door.

Windy entered the lounge wearing a leather bustier that matched her boots. "Cute little guys, aren't they!" she said to Kathy. "What a shame they have to grow up."

Kathy smiled sadly. "Indeed."

A few minutes later, at the ice cream shop, the two boys were digging into their hot fudge sundaes.

"Too bad we missed Windy's dance practice," Matt said.

Dorian licked his spoon. "Yeah. Do you think she would've taken off her clothes?"

Matt shrugged. "I dunno. I guess we'll have to grow up. Then we can go there and find out."

"Yeah, and then we'll understand." Dorian looked puzzled. "Um, what is it that we're s'posed to understand when we grow up?"

Matt shrugged again. "I dunno."

Sharky and The Fishermen

Lana looked in the dressing room mirror while her mother tied the sling up behind her neck. Through the thin material, she could see her wrist wrapped in bandages. She sighed. "Sharky is gonna freak!"

"Just because The Fishermen's fiddle player is out with a sprained wrist, and they're due on stage in half an hour?" Ma gave her a crooked smile. "Ya think?"

"Well, he's just going to have to take my place, isn't he? He's just as good a fiddle player as I am, if not better."

"Lana, he's always stayed in your shadow. Much as your Pa and I encouraged him, he never thought he could play that fiddle as well as you do." Ma took a sip of her water. "He's perfectly happy being your band's manager. He won't be too thrilled at the idea of taking your place."

Just then, there was a knock on the door. "Lana, you in there?" The door flew open and Sharky rushed in. "Half an hour to curtain call...." He stopped and stared at Lana's arm. "What's going on?"

"Oh Sharky, the most terrible thing happened. I tripped on the stairs and sprained my wrist! Ma just brought me here straight from the hospital."

Sharky looked concerned. "Are you okay? It's just a sprain?"

Lana nodded. "Yeah, it's not broken or anything, but I can't play tonight."

Sharky's concern changed to panic. "Oh good Lord, what are we going to do? The Fishermen need a fiddle player." He began to pace the room. "What kind of Celtic band doesn't have a fiddle player?"

Lana stepped in front of him. "Sharky, listen to me. You have to take my place."

Sharky blanched. "What! I can't do that! The audience is expecting you."

"The audience is expecting The Fishermen. They won't care who the fiddle player is!"

"But... but..." Sharky stared at Lana. "I'm not as good as you are."

Lana placed her free hand on her hip. "Sharky, all you have to do is play along with the band, like you do at our rehearsals. You know every note by heart!"

Sharky looked at Ma. She said, "We've always told you that you play as well as your sister. Now get out there and save the show!"

Sharky sighed, "Yes Ma." He left the room.

A few minutes later, Lana and Ma sat by the dressing room television and watched Sharky take the band to new heights with his fiddle-playing. Lana smiled. "I do believe we have a new band. Sharky and The Fishermen!"

"And that'll come in handy when you go on maternity leave, won't it." Ma nodded towards the screen. "I guess you'll have to tell Sharky and the other fellas soon."

"I will," Lana said. "But first, I'm going to have to deal with this little white lie." She took the sling off and began to unravel the bandages. She then shook out her perfectly healthy wrist.

Ma laughed. "I'm just glad I kept that old bedsheet. I knew it would come in handy for something. Although I never thought I'd be ripping it up into bandages so that my son could become a famous Celtic star!"

Lana laughed as well, and they sat back to watch the rest of the show.

The Cookie Recipe

It was after midnight, and the building was completely dark, thanks to the energy-conscious employees that spent their nine-to-fives here running high-powered equipment to make cookies, Kyle thought, and sending them all over the world. Yeah, Sugar Valley Bakery kept a lot of Sugar Valley folks in jobs. Except him.

He and his partner-in-crime, Shags, were standing outside the VP's office door. Partner-in-crime? No no, not a crime, really. He was just going to get his recipe back. It wasn't a crime taking back what was yours, was it?

"Hey Kyle, are you gonna pick this lock, or what?" Shags whispered.

Kyle shook off his reverie. "Yeah, yeah. And you don't need to whisper. There isn't a soul in sight." He pulled out his pick and went to work. "You got your gloves on?"

Shags nervously scratched his namesake wildly-curly head. "Yeah. Hey, you sure you took care of the alarm?"

Kyle sighed. Shags was his childhood buddy and current roommate, but he could be a pain in the brain sometimes. Thankfully, Kyle had enough brain for the both of them. "Yeah, I know the code, remember? Now can it, will ya! And stop scratching your head! That habit of yours drives me batty!"

"Okay, sure." Shags scratched his head again.

Kyle fussed with the lock until it clicked. "There we go," he said and opened the door. They stepped inside and slowly moved their flashlights around the office. A tidy desk stood in the centre of the room, surrounded by several cushy chairs. There was a single window behind the desk.

Kyle went over to it and pulled the blind down. He reached for the desk lamp and turned it on.

Shags looked around. "All the years you've worked here, and I've never seen this place."

"You never had a reason to come here, I guess. I always brought cookies home for you." Kyle shrugged. "This wasn't my office anyway. I was in the bullpen, coming up with marketing ideas." His voice became icy. "Like the recipe they stole from me."

"You should've kept a copy of it," Shags said.

"I wouldn't've had to if I still had my job, Shaggy-boy! I just wanted a nice fat bonus for it, but they canned me instead!" Kyle moved towards the wall and moved a family photo, exposing a small safe. "Now, if I'm not mistaken, the VP had planned to keep it tucked away safely until they were ready to get a patent on it just before marketing it. If I can get it back, I can patent it first!" He began to turn the combination lock. After a couple of turns, it clicked open. "Yes! He didn't even change the combination!" He looked through all the papers, but didn't find what he was looking for. "Dang, it's not here!"

Shags moved towards the desk. "What are we looking for?" he asked as he opened a drawer.

Kyle closed the safe, replaced the photo, and sat down at the computer. "Be careful, Shags! I don't want to leave a mess behind!"

"Sure Kyle." Shags dumped the contents of a drawer on the floor and scratched his head.

Kyle sighed. "Okay, just look for a mini-disc with "Cranberry Sauerkraut Crunch" written on it.

Shags stopped what he was doing. "Sauerkraut? Ewwww!"

"Never mind! Just find it!"

Shags opened another drawer. "Hey Kyle, look!" He took out a package of cookies. "Double Sunflower Smiles! I haven't had one of these in a long time!" He opened the package and took a cookie out.

"What are you doing?" Kyle yelled. "I told you not to leave a mess!"

Shags munched on the cookie. "I'm not!" he mumbled. "I plan to eat every crumb!"

Kyle sighed and rubbed his eyes. "I don't see the recipe on the computer. I suppose that's a good thing; it means he hasn't transferred a copy yet." He got up and began to pace around the office. "Where the heck is that disc?"

Shags reached into the bag for another cookie and bit into it. "Hey!" He pulled the cookie out of his mouth and looked at it. "Um, Kyle..."

"Quiet! I'm thinking!"

Shags scratched his head. "But..."

"I said shut-up!"

"No, you shut-up!" Shags hollered, and then covered his mouth with his cookie-filled hand. "Sorry Kyle, I didn't mean it."

Kyle was staring at the cookie in his hand. "Ah, Shags..." He moved toward Shags.

Shags stepped back. "I said I was sorry!"

"Never mind that!" Kyle pulled the cookie out of Shags' hand and looked at it. The half-eaten cookie revealed something shiny inside. He broke off the rest of the cookie and began to laugh.

"What's so funny?" Shags said.

"We did it!" Kyle held up a small computer disc. "We found my recipe! It was shoved inside a cookie, of all places!"

He grabbed Shags by the shoulders and plopped a big kiss on his cheek.

Shags jumped away and began rubbing his cheek vigorously. "Ew, that was gross!"

Still laughing, Kyle slapped his friend on the shoulder. "I knew I kept you around for something!" He tucked the disc safely into his pocket. "Now, let's clean up and get out of here."

"Can I take these cookies with me?" Shags asked.

Kyle laughed again. "Sure, why not. Might as well eat the evidence."

They took a few minutes to put everything back as it was, and then slipped out of the office. At the main door, Kyle reset the alarm and they left the building.

As they headed home, Kyle patted the disc in his pocket and said, "I'll make you a batch of these as soon as we get back home. You'll love 'em!"

Shags gulped. "Yeah. Sauerkraut." He scratched his head, and for once, it didn't annoy Kyle.

The Dignity of Surgery

"Okay Mrs N, please disrobe completely and put your dignity in this bag."

I blinked at the nurse. "Pardon me?"

"Your clothes; please put them in this bag." She handed me a couple of hospital gowns; you know the kind. "Put the blue one on with the opening at the back and put the green one on like a housecoat."

I vaguely wondered if anybody ever wore their housecoat backwards, like one of those snuggie blankets with the arms, and whether the owner of such a blanket had ever proclaimed that he was indeed wearing the outer gown like a housecoat and he couldn't help it if his bum was bare. Then I wondered if any exhibitionists ever wore the gowns that way on purpose and got away with it because, well gosh darn, they're hospital gowns!

I quickly changed and made sure my two gowns were on the right way. I might as well salvage what little dignity I had left, I thought, seeing as I packed most of it away in a bag that would end up sitting in the corner of my hospital room for the next four days while I sported that stylish open-back gown.

Oh well, such is the dignity of surgery. You don't get to bring much of it with you when you go for the surgery, but then again, dignity is the last thing on your mind. You just want everything to go well, and considering the fact that you're letting a team of doctors and nurses (most of whom you've never even met before) rip you open, that's not much to ask for.

It doesn't matter that a stranger is going to put you into a coma. It doesn't matter that another is going to shove a tube down your throat and control your breathing. You try not to think of the fact that your legs are going to be in stirrups; as a woman, that position has become a given. But you do strike one up for dignity if you remembered to shave your legs that morning. And don't forget the fact that you have met your surgeon at least once or twice and she'll be the one who'll slice you open and sew you up again. Of course, I'm not sure about the sewing you up again part. I've watched enough television to know that at least two members of the OR team are having, or have had an affair and are probably arguing over your comatose body. And surely the assisting surgeon is having a meltdown because her love life is going nowhere. And with my luck, she'll be the one to sew me up because my head surgeon probably has to run off to call her bookie.

(Noticed that I keep saying "she"? That's right, my whole OR team consisted of women. It seems more and more women are opting for careers in the medical field. Just a little info for the guys to maul over the next time THEY find themselves knees up in a pair of stirrups.)

Ever notice how a doctor will always say "The procedure is simple"? Of course it is; years of medical training allow her to say that and actually mean it. What she fails to mention is the fact that while the procedure is simple, the recovery is pure hell. And no matter how prepared you are for it, you wake up from the surgery feeling like you've been stabbed in the gut (and chances are you have been). Of course, you're sporting an IV with a morphine drip, so who cares if you have a large cut across your abdomen and a catheter draining you of even more dignity, just when you thought you didn't have any left.

That's the nice thing about painkillers; they can dull all kinds of pain. It doesn't matter that the main topic of conversation for the next few days will be your bodily functions. You're in the hospital, you're high on Tylenol 3s and you've nothing else to do but worry about your pee bag (which you giddily show off to your visitors) or whether you're going to overflow your barf bowl (I won't even go there).

But you know what seems to be the most exciting bodily function when you're in the hospital? Passing gas! You have to hand it to nurses; what other profession can allow you to thoroughly discuss farting with your clients? "Now Mrs. N, it's very important for you to pass gas. You cannot eat until you pass gas. You cannot lose the IV until you pass gas. You cannot leave the hospital until you pass gas." Imagine being held hostage by a bodily function.

"No prob, Nurse!" you say in your drugged stupor. "Yer lookin' at a pro!"

I know, right? You're lying in a hospital bed in a room with three other women who've probably been told the same thing. You patiently wait for your bowels to co-operate while vaguely wondering why you're not hearing any gassy noises coming from your roommates. Soon the gas pains set in and they join all the other abdominal pains so that it becomes absolute agony to let go of that treasured gas bubble. Ah, finally... oops, that was noisy... I hope the other ladies didn't hear that... It sucks to be a woman sometimes. I bet all the guys in the men's wards are having contests on who can fart the loudest! No matter; now I have something to brag to the nurses about. Now I can eat!

Which brings us to hospital food. It really isn't that bad, although I think the passing gas thing is a ruse to starve us so that we actually look forward to the food. Of course, when you haven't eaten for three days, cream of broccoli soup isn't exactly the first thing you want to pour down your throat. But hey, the crackers were good! And by the last day, I was actually enjoying the meatloaf!

So there's my four-day hospital stay wrapped up in a dignity-free blanket. My catheter came out after a couple of days (at least I was able to show it off to most of my visitors first) and I got to pee in a measuring cup. Well, a big one anyway. Hey, we have to measure our dignity somehow! I guess 200cc's of dignity, er, pee is a good sign that all is going well. By the fourth day I was able to take the rest of my dignity out of the clothes bag in the corner of the room, get dressed and leave the hospital on schedule.

There's just one thing I always wonder about hospital stays. Why do they wake you up to give you a sleeping pill?

Family Affairs

A Dream Come True

She stares at the screen and the screen stares back. Nothing comes to her. How can it? The voices in the background are getting louder.

"Honey, have you seen my belt?"

"Mom, what's there to eat?"

She has an hour. Her deadline is in an hour and she has nothing.

Now the voices are directed at each other. They're talking about auto parts. And they're doing it in the computer room.

"Guys, please!" she yells.

They both saunter over to her. "What's the problem?"

"Nothing! That's the problem!" She loses her temper. "I need a dream to come true, and right now that dream would be for both of you to disappear!"

She pushes her seat back a little too quickly and topples over, hitting her head. Moments, or maybe hours later, she wakes up. She shakes her head and looks around.

"Ah, guys, a little help here!" But no one comes to help. She gives herself a moment, and then gets up. "Well, at least they disappeared for a while."

She walks around the house to loosen up her sore muscles. She glances at the closet, and sees only her coat and jacket hanging there. She looks down and sees only her shoes. Now why on earth would they take all of their stuff with them, she wonders.

She goes into the kitchen. Her son's CD player is missing, as is her husband's HAM radio. Took their noise with them too! She opens the fridge to get a cold drink. It's almost bare! All of her son's favourite food is gone. She takes a sniff and notices the familiar reek of her husband's provolone cheese is missing.

Head hurting from the fall and dizzy with confusion, she takes a few breaths. Something is wrong here. She runs up the stairs and into her son's room. The furniture is there, but there is no trace of her son. No clothes in the closet (or on the floor), no books, no CD's, no posters of Christina Aguilera on the wall.

Heart pounding, she runs to her room. She sees traces of her own existence but none of her husband's. She feels faint and sits on the bed. She picks up her husband's pillow and puts it to her face. The familiar faint smell of her husband's cologne is no longer there.

She begins to giggle. Slowly the giggle turns to laughter. Good grief! They really disappeared! But how did they do that so fast? I was only out for a few minutes. The nervous laughter turns to sobbing. No, please, I want them back! She cries uncontrollably for a few minutes, then falls into a restless sleep.

She wakes up a few hours later, jogs her memory, and once again panics. "No!" she yells.

"What's wrong?" Her husband runs into the room. "Are you okay?"

"What?"

"Mom, what is it?" Her son pokes his head in. "You've been asleep for quite a while; are you all right?"

She starts to laugh. "I'm just fine. I, uh, was having a dream about a dream that came true."

The two men in her life look at each other and shrug. They then turn their conversation to auto parts.

Antonio and the Cow

"The Germans are coming, the Germans are coming!"

Those dreaded words sent chills up Antonio's spine. He knew it would happen soon enough. The German army was sweeping through Europe, and now that Italy was no longer its ally, the inevitable had happened.

And Antonio was not at home with his family. He and his son Giovanni had ridden into town with some neighbouring farmers to sell some goods at the market.

"Papa, we have to get home!" Giovanni exclaimed. They began packing their things, as did the other farmers, and loaded up the truck. Soon they were on their way back to their small farming community, one of many in the northern Venetian region.

On the way back, traffic slowed down and they noticed several army trucks loaded with soldiers driving by, their first glimpse at what was to be a common sight for the next several years. As they passed farms, they noticed similar trucks parked next to barns. Animals were being loaded into the trucks. They could hear shouting and crying, no doubt by the farmers and their families. Antonio swallowed the lump in his throat as they continued their slow trek home.

As they entered their village, the sense of panic increased. There seemed to be no German soldiers in sight, but barnyards seemed to lack the bustle of chickens and ducks, and the fields were empty of grazing cows. Farmers and their families, who were usually busy with Saturday afternoon chores, were just standing around, some dazed, some crying, many angered.

Antonio and Giovanni were the first ones to be dropped off. They hurried down the lane, their market goods forgotten and left by the roadside. Antonio was relieved to see his wife and children safely standing outside the house.

His wife Paola, saw him and burst into tears. "They took everything," she sobbed.

He looked at his four daughters, three sons and two daughter-in-laws. They looked shocked, but unharmed. He had to make sure. "Was anyone hurt?"

Everyone shook their heads to some degree. "We're fine," Paola verified. "But they took all of our animals. What are we going to do?" She burst into fresh tears.

Not being an affectionate type, Antonio awkwardly gathered her into his arms. "My family is safe," he told her. "That's the important part."

Paola looked up at him through teary eyes. "They took Mora."

Antonio closed his eyes and nodded. "I was afraid of that." He looked over at the open doors of the barn. The eerie silence swept over him. No chickens clucking in the yard. No occasional moo coming from the barn. And no Mora.

He felt a sudden anger sweep over him. "Giovanni, get everyone into the house. The Germans have taken what they wanted, so you should all be safe. But keep the rifle handy in case the odd one comes back to cause trouble." He turned around and headed towards the village, oblivious to his family's questions and worries.

Unsure of where he was going, he slowed his pace and thought about Mora. She was born on a cold winter's night in the warmth of the barn. Her mother, an aging cow, died from the birth. When the other cows refused to nurse her, Antonio used a nursing bottle borrowed from a neighbouring farmer and did the job himself. She quickly grew into a sprite young calf. Her colouring was much darker than the other tan cows, so he named her Mora, an Italian slang word for "dark one". His family and friends teased him about his pet cow, but there was a unique relationship between himself and Mora. And he knew he had to get her back.

As he entered the village, he noticed a strange hush that swept over the usually bustling centre. All the villagers had gone home, obviously fearing what was to become of their happy homes. German soldiers were roaming the streets. So far, he hadn't seen any violence, and he felt hopeful that these boys were merely here to do their jobs and not cause unnecessary trouble. And hopefully the villagers would keep their hotheaded Italian tempers in check and equally not cause trouble.

A few young soldiers were sitting along the fountain, smoking cigarettes. Antonio gathered up his courage and walked over to them. "Parlate Italiano?"

One of the soldiers stood. "I speak Italian," he said in the same language. "What would you like?"

"I would like to know what became of our animals," Antonio answered.

"What does it matter?" the soldier said. "They belong to us now."

Antonio nodded. "I know. But there is one animal in particular I'd like back."

The soldier shrugged. "That would be impossible. But I'll tell you what. Get me some cigarettes, and I'll show you where we're keeping the animals."

Antonio reached into his pocket, where he kept a nearly full pack, and handed it to the soldier. "There's more where that came from. I had planned to quit smoking anyway."

The soldier chuckled. "Come with me, Signore." He said something in German to his comrades and then led Antonio out of the village centre.

They walked out into the countryside, both keeping silent for the half hour it took to reach the farm with the large silo. Antonio recognized the farm as one of the more successful ones in the area. He didn't know the farmer well, but he couldn't help feeling sorry for him. The whole farm was taken over by the Germans. There were hundreds of animals there, both inside and outside of the various barns.

The young soldier brought Antonio over to a small group of soldiers and spoke with them. An older one, whom Antonio figured was some sort of sergeant, turned to him and spoke in Italian.

"You're looking for a certain animal?" he asked.

"Yes," Antonio gulped and continued. "You see, she's not just a farm cow. She's sort of a pet. Her name is Mora"

The sergeant looked at him. "You have a pet cow."

Antonio nodded.

The sergeant said something in German to the other soldiers. They all looked at Antonio for a moment. Then they all burst out laughing.

Antonio hung his head in dismay. Not only did he feel foolish, but he now knew he would never see Mora again.

The sergeant amicably slapped Antonio on the back. "My friend, we have hundreds of cows here. If you can find your Mora, you can have her."

Relief washed over Antonio. He began to walk through the barnyard, with the still chuckling soldiers in tow. He looked at all of the cows and began to panic. They all looked like Mora. He'd have to get close up to each one of them to recognize her. Even with her dark colouring, it would take forever.

There was only one way he could do this. "Mora!" he called out in a singsong voice. "Yoohoo, Mora!" The soldiers began to laugh again. This only made Antonio more determined. He went to the largest barn and stood in the doorway. "Mora, Mora!" he sang loudly.

Suddenly there was a loud mooing, and a cow began to charge through the barn. She reached the doorway and trotted over to Antonio. "Mora!" he yelled out happily, and threw his arms around her neck. He didn't notice that the soldiers had stopped laughing.

He turned to the sergeant. "This is Mora," he said. "May I take her home?"

The sergeant smiled, as did the other soldiers. "I've never seen anything like it," the sergeant said. "Cows are usually stupid."

Antonio smiled. "They aren't stupid. They are just passive."

The sergeant nodded. "Take her home," he said.

As Antonio turned to leave, the sergeant yelled out, "Wait a minute!" He went to gather up some animals, and came back, handing Antonio a small cage with some chickens, and the reins to two more cows. "Take this home to your family." The sergeant walked away, as did the other soldiers, except the young man who had accompanied Antonio. He noticed tears in the young soldier's eyes.

"I owe you some cigarettes, "Antonio told him as they headed out of the farm, animals in tow.

The soldier shook his head. He wiped the tears from his eyes. "You remind me of my father. He has the same kind of relationship with animals as you do. Only the kindest of hearts can weave that kind of magic." He took the chickens from Antonio and carried them.

When they reached the village, he handed the chickens back to Antonio.

"Thank you," Antonio said.

"No, thank you!" the soldier answered. He turned and walked away.

Mora mooed. Antonio smiled. "Yes my friend, we're going home."

Antonio made his way back to his farm with his animals.

(Dedicated to my grandparents Antonio and Paola, and their pet cow, Mora.)

April in Italy

"Are you all set to go, Mama?" I loaded the large suitcase into the trunk of the car while my mother settled into the front seat.

"Si, we go!" She smiled at me as I got in and set the car in motion. I began to smile back, but froze as I looked at the necklace around her neck.

"Hey, that's my cross! I want it back!"

"No no, I take!" Mama wrapped her frail hand around the small gold cross... my gold cross. "I take! It keep me safe in airplane!"

"But Mama..." I felt defeated. That cross once belonged to my sister. She had given it to me when we were teenagers; she was dying of leukaemia, and I was at her bedside constantly, a part of me dying with her. She had taken the cross from her neck and placed it in my hand. "Perhaps it will keep you safer than it did me," she had said.

How could I tell Mama that she couldn't take her daughter's cross to Italy with her?

Dear sweet Mama. She and Papa came to Canada shortly before my twin sister and I were born. Papa died a couple of years after my sister did, and our family soon dwindled down to the two of us. Then I got married, and she was alone, albeit not lonely. She began to travel, and she made a point of spending every April in Italy. She had many friends and relatives there, but I've always suspected she had her share of boyfriends there too.

"I no have boyfriend!" She would always blush when I teased her about it. "I too old!"

"You're not old, Mama," I would assure her. "And you're still beautiful!" And that was true. Mama took good care of herself. She was 70 going on 50.

She was never able to master the English language, and her side of the conversation always consisted of short, clipped phrases. Oh, it wasn't for lack of trying; she was very proud of what English she could master. From the moment she stepped onto Canadian soil, her ears were open to those who spoke English around her.

She would always chuckle whenever she told me about her first English words. She was aboard the train from Halifax, and there was a fellow in her compartment who was trying to get some sleep. Apparently, he kept hitting his head on the side of the compartment because of the bumpy ride, and the same expletive phrase kept popping out of his mouth. From then on, my mother would proudly exclaim that the first English words she ever learned were, "Sona ma beech!"

Now, I was driving her to the airport so that she could spend yet another April in Italy. This was her first trip abroad since the 9/11 disaster, which had put the fear of flying into her, but with a little reassurance from me, and much coaxing from her friends in Italy, she was well on her way to travelling again.

Watching her go through the security check would be quite interesting, if not comical.

We got her flight verified and her luggage checked in without incident. As she watched her suitcase being tagged, she hugged her large carry-on bag. "I take!" she told the clerk, who only smiled at her.

We reached the departure gates, and I hugged her good-bye. I watched through the window as she passed the various security measures. Then the comedy began.

She was asked to remove her shoes.

"No no! I take!"

She was asked again.

"No no! I take!"

"Mama, just take your shoes off! You'll get them back!" I yelled in Italian through the window, although I doubted she heard me.

Another security guard reached for her bag. Mama clung to it.

"No no! I take!"

The guard gripped her bag and pulled it. Mama pulled back. After a brief tug-of-war, two more security guards surrounded her.

I simply stared through the window as four big men wrestled a little old lady to the ground; all the while she was kicking and screaming, "Sona ma beech!"

When they picked her back up again, she looked through the window, pointed at me, and said, "You talka to my daughter!"

Moments later, I felt two sets of strong hands grip my arms and drag me away.

I found myself in a room with my purseless, shoeless and somewhat dishevelled mother and two very tough-looking female guards. I paled as I realized why they were there.

"Are you going to, ah, search my mother?" I asked them.

"Only if she gives us reason to," They both smiled, which softened their formidable features, although not enough to put me at ease. Then one of them turned to my mother and began to speak to her in Italian.

After several minutes of questions and explanations, the guards were satisfied that my mother misunderstood the security check. They escorted us back to the departure gate with only minutes left before the plane would take off. We were allowed a quick hug before one of the guards would escort my mother through the security check.

After we hugged, she reached around her neck, took the gold cross off and held it out for me. I took it, and put it back around her neck.

"No no," I said to her as I closed the clasp on it. "You take!"

"Si, I take." She smiled at me. Then she went through the boarding gate and into her April in Italy.

Dave

Kate nibbled on her lip as she dialled her mother's number. "Mom? Have you seen Dave?"

There was a moment of silence. "Dave? Why on earth would I see Dave? Kate, what's wrong?"

Kate started to cry. "He's gone! I came home from work two days ago, and he wasn't here."

"Oh now, honey, take it easy. Have you checked with your neighbours? Dave is quite popular with the folks there."

"Yes, I looked for him everywhere," Kate sobbed. "I think he might've left me. I've been warned about his wanderlust, but I wouldn't believe it."

"But Dave loves you so, dear." Another moment of silence. "Kate, I hope nothing happened to him."

Kate nodded at the phone. "Me too. Anyway, I was grasping for straws when I called you. I realize Dave doesn't even know where you live, never mind making the 200 mile trip to visit you."

Just as Kate hung up the phone, her cell phone beeped a text message. She picked it up and read the message. "I have the money and hid the body." Her angst turned to anger. She didn't recognize the phone number, but as an undercover cop, Simon changed his cell phones frequently. She decided to call his office directly.

Simon barely picked up the phone when Kate spat out, "How could you be so cruel? Well great, you have the divorce settlement finalized! Hooray, the money is in the bank! Oh, and by the way, Kate, I murdered Dave and hid his body!" Kate burst into tears again. "Simon, that is not funny!"

There was a moment of silence. There seemed to be a lot of silent moments, Kate thought, but the worst was the silence of her house without Dave there.

Simon broke into her thoughts. "What the heck are you babbling about, Kate? First of all, the sale of our old house hasn't been finalized yet, so no, there is no money. And second of all, what do you mean, I murdered Dave?"

"Dave has been gone for a couple of days." Kate wiped her tears.

"And you think I killed him?" Simon asked incredulously. "Kate, you know me better than that. The last thing I'd do is murder the new love of your life. Besides, our marriage fell apart long before Dave came on the scene, so I have no reason to be jealous."

Kate sighed. "You're right. I'm sorry. But I got this text message, and I thought... well, I just didn't know what to think." She went on to explain the text message.

"Kate, don't delete that message." Simon told her. "Can you bring your phone here? There may be a connection to a case we're working on, and it may be crucial evidence."

"Sure," Kate said, "But what about Dave?"

Simon sighed. "You know, Kate, I heard he's a bit of a wanderer. Maybe he's just gone."

"Thanks a lot," Kate answered through gritted teeth. She gave Simon the caller's phone number so that he could begin looking into it, then she left the house to bring him the phone.

She decided to walk to the police station. It gave her time to think things over. Simon was a good cop, and she knew he could never have done anything to Dave, no matter how jealous he might be. Her thoughts then turned to Dave. He'd had a rough life; subjected to abuse when he was a little guy, he ran off and ended up in a foster home. He was treated well there, but he still tried to run away. He later had a string of kind, warm-hearted ladies in his life, but still he ran. And then he met Kate. She swore it was love at first sight. On her part, anyway.

Kate sighed. Oh, who am I kidding, she thought. Once a wanderer, always a wanderer. Maybe he was ready to move on. She smiled sadly. Well, at least he wasn't the body in the phone message.

Fifteen minutes later, she was sitting in Simon's office. Simon had given the phone number to a detective who was working on a mob case. They had already traced the number to an individual, believed to be connected to the mob ring in question.

"Some mobsters aren't very smart," Simon commented to Kate. "Not very lucky either. Imagine dialling a wrong number and getting a cop's ex-wife!" He whisked her cell phone over the detective, then came back and sat down across the desk from Kate.

"Sorry about the phone," Simon said. "I'll get you another one."

"Thanks," Kate said. "Now, what should I do about finding Dave?"

"I have connections. I'll see what I can do for you."

Kate smiled. "Thank you, Simon." She got up to leave. "But I think you're right. Dave left me. Now that I look back at it, he's been a bit down the last few days. I couldn't figure out what was wrong. Now it all makes sense."

Simon surprised her with a hug. "I'm sorry, Kate." He kept his arms around her, and she settled into the comfortable hug she missed so much from him. "Our marriage may have died out, but I do want you to be happy.

And I know how much you love Dave." He let go of her. She smiled at him and left the office.

A few minutes later, she was walking up her driveway, her head down in deep thought. Her head snapped up at the sound of the familiar grunt. She froze in place for a moment. "Dave?" she whispered. "Dave?" she shouted. She leaped towards the big, black figure sitting on the front porch, threw her arms around him and nuzzled her face into the handsome ebony face. "Oh Dave," she sobbed.

Dave looked into Kate's eyes, and then gave her face a big, slobbery lick, all the while wagging his tail furiously. He then jumped up, placed his paws on her shoulders, knocked her into the flower garden with all the strength a black lab could muster, and fell on top of her. Kate laughed. She lay there for a few minutes with her arms around her dog. "Welcome home, Dave," she said. "Welcome home."

Explosions in the Night

"Oh, how I envy your youth," I tell my daughter Chris as she adds the finishing touches to herself with a spritz of perfume. "Here I am getting ready for bed, and here you are getting ready for a night on the town."

"I'm going to Explosions," she tells me.

"Explosions?" I give her a baffled look. "You're going to see fireworks this time of night?"

"No Mom!" Chris rolls her eyes. "That's the name of the club I'm going to."

"Oh, you joined a club? What kind of club is it? And why would you be meeting so late?"

"Mother!" I know I'm in trouble when my kids call me Mother.

"Well, you tell me you're going to a club called Explosions. Sounds like you're going to learn how to make bombs or something."

Chris sighs. "Okay, Mom, listen carefully. You used to call them discos. We now call them clubs. You used to go bar-hopping. We now go clubbing."

"Clubbing?" I giggle. "Sounds like a cave man thing. Is that how you girls catch your men these days?" I start to chuckle. "Yeah, I could think of a few fellas that deserved a good clubbing back in my days."

"Very funny," Chris grabs her purse. "Well, I'm ready. I just have to wait for my ride."

I look at her outfit. Or lack of it. Tight jeans and a very small camisole. "Uh, I think you forgot to get dressed."

"I am dressed."

"No, you're not. You're in your underwear."

Chris gives me a long look. She then turns around and goes back to her room. Moments later, she emerges with a photo album in her hands. "I found this picture the other day."

"Oh," I can feel my cheeks turn red. She shows me a photo of myself twenty-five years ago, dressed for a night out. Or should I say, not quite dressed.

A car horn sounds outside. "Saved by the horn!" Chris hands me the photo album.

"Have fun at Explosions," I call after her. I close the door behind her and proceed to look through the album. After a few minutes of nostalgia, I close the album and head up to bed.

As I approach the bedroom, I can hear my husband snoring. And I can hear some noises coming from his opposite end. I sigh as I realize that I am going to my own kind of Explosions tonight... just like every night.

The Fitting Rooms

The elderly man and the teenaged girl are standing in line in the Navy Blue store, awaiting a fitting room on a busy Saturday afternoon. The man looks out of place as he glances around the popular clothing store. The girl looks a little uncomfortable, but smiles at him.

"You don't have to wait in line with me, Grampa. I know you like walking around the mall. We could meet up later."

"That's okay Mandy, I don't mind." He shakes his head. He is hard of hearing and tends to speak loudly. "Someone aughta turn that music down. It's so loud even I can hear it!"

Amanda looks embarrassed. "Shh, Grampa, everyone will hear you."

"How can anyone hear me with this music playing so loud!" He looks down at his granddaughter and lowers his voice. "I'm sorry, Mandy, I didn't mean to embarrass you. Maybe I'll go for that walk after all."

Amanda gives him a sheepish look. "Oh no Grampa, it's okay. I don't mind if you wait here with me. After all, you were nice enough to drive me here."

Grampa smiles back at her. "I'll try not to embarrass you." He looks up and down the line-up and sees a teenaged boy in line behind him. He raises his voice once again. "Hey young man, you're in the wrong line. This is the ladies' fitting rooms."

The boy stares at him.

Grampa chuckles. "Oh I must've confused you. I'm not in line, I'm just waiting for my granddaughter here." He points to Amanda, who is now beet red with embarrassment. The boy smiles at her.

"Grampa," she hisses. "He's in the right line-up. There are no other fitting rooms."

"What? They never built fitting rooms for men here? What kind of place is this?"

"Shh, Grampa, keep it down. A lot of these stores have unisex fitting rooms these days."

"Sheesh, this is almost as bad as that television show with the unisex bathroom! Why, when I was young..."

Amanda interrupts him. "Um, I'm next in line, Grampa. I'll just be a few minutes trying on these jeans."

"Okay Mandy." He spots an attractive elderly lady waiting just outside the fitting rooms. He winks at his granddaughter. "I'll just go flirt, er, I mean talk to that lady over there. Maybe she's widowed like I am."

Amanda giggles. "You go, Grampa!" With that, she disappears into one of the rooms.

Grampa casually strolls over and stands next to the lady. They nod hello to each other and he says, "So, do you come here often?"

The lady laughs. "Only when my grandson insists on shopping for clothes." She points towards the fitting rooms. "He's the young man who was standing behind you." She gives him a knowing look. "You know, the one who has to use the ladies' fitting rooms."

They both laugh and she introduces herself as Rachel. They spend a few minutes chatting. After a while, Grampa wonders what is taking Amanda so long. He excuses himself and goes into the fitting rooms. He doesn't realize that he passes right by Amanda, who is just outside the fitting room cubicles talking to Rachel's grandson.

"Mandy?" he begins to call loudly. "Mandy, are you in here?" He proceeds to look under the fitting room doors, in hopes of recognizing his granddaughter's feet. What he doesn't realize is that he is causing a stir as he draws gasps and screams from all the people in the fitting room cubicles. "Mandy?" He sees a pair of feet wearing what looks like Amanda's shoes. "Oh there you are. What's taking you so long?" He begins to knock on the fitting room door, causing the occupant to scream.

By now, the staff has called Security and Amanda is standing behind her grandfather in shock. "Grampa, what are you doing?"

Grampa turns around. "Oh Mandy, there you are."

A hand grips his arm. "Come with me, Sir," a big, burly security guard begins to escort him out.

"No no, it's alright," Amanda explains. "This is my Grampa. He was just looking for me."

"That's right," Grampa turns to Amanda. "I kept thinking I found you. Do you know how many girls wear thongs like yours?"

Amanda gasps. "Grampa!"

The security guard gives him a steely look. "You were looking at women in their thongs? And how would you know about your granddaughter's, ah..."

"I may be deaf, but I'm not blind!" He points to Amanda's sandal-clad feet. "See? All the girls wear those things these days!"

"Oh Grampa." Amanda giggles. "These aren't called thongs any more. They're flip-flops, or maybe thong sandals, but not just thongs. Thongs are, well, underwear."

Grampa looks at Amanda's sandals. "How can anybody wear those things as underwear?"

The security guard tries to keep a straight face as he looks at the seemingly harmless elderly man. Then he looks at the young girl. "He was causing quite a disturbance," he says to Amanda. He gives her a sympathetic look. "He kinda reminds me of my Granddad. Look, why don't you just take him out of here. And make sure he doesn't come into this store for a little while."

"Yes sir, and thanks." Amanda hooks her arm into Grampa's and leads him to the exit.

"Sheesh, what a big deal!" Grampa begins to rant loudly. "Like I was a pervert or something!" He notices Rachel on the way out. She seems amused and gives him a big smile.

Grampa chuckles. He turns to Amanda. "Oh well, at least your old grandfather still has what it takes. Look what I got." He shows her a slip of paper with Rachel's phone number on it.

Amanda laughs. "I guess that charm runs in the family. Look!" She shows him a slip of paper with the same phone number. "His name is Jamie. He lives with his grandmother."

"Great!" Grampa chuckles. "Maybe we can go on a double date!"

Amanda rolls her eyes. "Or maybe not!"

The elderly man and the teenaged girl exit the mall laughing.

The Lifejacket

Prologue

The writer stood in front of St. Peter. She was anxious to get through the Pearly Gates, but she could see it wasn't going to be easy...

"You've been very naughty," St. Peter was telling her. "Not bad, just naughty. Bad gets you a one-way trip down the escalator. Naughty gives you a second chance. This is what you must do to earn your way into Heaven... You will be re-incarnated. Animal, vegetable, or mineral, but not human. And since you are an imaginative writer, what you do with this is up to you..."

The Lifejacket

The little girl sat on the steps that led below deck. It had started to rain, and she could feel the boat rocking as the wind picked up. She ran her hand along her lifejacket. What did Daddy call it? Oh yeah, a PFD, whatever that was. She could hear her parents arguing about it on deck...

"Why do you have to call it a Personal Flotation Device? Can't you just call it a lifejacket like everyone else?" Daria's face was red with anger. "You always have to be a hotshot, don't you!"

"It's the way I've been trained. I tend to use technical phrases sometimes. Is that so bad?" Kevin spoke calmly in contrast to his wife's temper. His self-control gave him the edge as a sharp Coast Guard Officer. He held out Daria's lifejacket. "Now, will you put this on? It's really starting to get choppy out here and I've got to get us back to shore."

"You're so smart, it's amazing you didn't predict this storm!" Daria refused to take the lifejacket.

"Don't get sarcastic. Sometimes these storms come up quickly, and you know it!" Kevin sighed in exasperation. "I can't understand why you won't wear this thing when we're out here. You know it only takes a moment for something to happen!"

Daria crossed her arms. "Maybe I just don't want to give you the satisfaction." She took the lifejacket from Kevin, but didn't put it on. She sat quietly for a few minutes as Kevin expertly steered the boat through the storm. She looked up at the dark sky. The warm rain felt good on her face. "At least there's no lightening... yet."

"Just a terribly strong wind. That's what I'm worried about." He looked at Daria. "This is getting really bad between us. What are we going to do?"

Daria shook her head. "If it wasn't for Jaclyn, I'd say our marriage was over."

"I think our marriage is over, regardless of Jaclyn."

Kevin looked towards the stairs. He didn't see his seven-year-old daughter sitting there, crying. She didn't quite understand what divorce was, but it had something to do with a Mommy and a Daddy not living together any more. Her friend Jessica had divorced parents, and they had to take turns with Jessica. Jaclyn wanted her parents to be together. But they have been fighting for a long time, and sometimes about her too.

She had a great idea. She would tell her parents that she would be a good girl from now on. Maybe then they will stay together. She got up and began to climb the steps, when the boat suddenly jolted and threw her backwards below deck. She felt herself bounce heavily, and then the boat settled. She got up and felt a little dazed. Her family has had this boat throughout her short life, and she recognized the fact that they had just met up with a strong wave. She ran upstairs to see if her parents were okay.

The first thing she noticed was that Daddy wasn't steering the boat. In fact, he was lying on the deck, unconscious. Her Mommy was nowhere to be seen.

She went over to Kevin. "Daddy... Daddy, wake up! Where's Mommy?" She then noticed a gash on his head. "Daddy, you're bleeding... wake up!"

Jaclyn held back her tears. She remembered what Daddy taught her to do if there was ever a problem and she was afraid. She went over to the radio. "May Day, May Day, May Day... Please help us. My Daddy is hurt and I can't find my Mommy!"

A nice man spent a few moments talking to her. She told him Kevin's name, and he recognized him as a Coast Guard Officer. He told her to look in the water for her Mommy.

As Jaclyn began to look over the water, she was drawn to the back of the boat. There, she saw her Mommy's lifejacket. She felt herself panic as she realized Mommy was in the water without it. She picked it up as she scanned the water once more.

She thought she could hear her name cutting through the strong wind. She followed the sound and saw her mother in the water fighting the large waves. "Jaclyn, the lifejacket!"

"Mommy!" Jaclyn thought she felt the lifejacket move. She looked down at it, and saw it flapping in the wind. She raised it as high as her little arms could lift it and threw it towards her Mommy. The wind picked it up and sent it in the opposite direction. "Oh no!"

She could see Mommy trying to swim towards it, but she kept going under the water. She was so afraid that Mommy was going to drown, and began to cry. Suddenly, the wayward lifejacket began to float towards her Mommy. "Mommy, look! Get the lifejacket!"

Daria was exhausted from trying to swim through the rough water. She felt herself sinking and knew she was about to die. The sound of her daughter's voice gave her a second wind and she noticed the lifejacket floating towards her. She regained her strength and swam the few feet she needed to reach it. She quickly grabbed it and awkwardly slipped into it, just as a Coast Guard boat pulled up.

A few hours later, Kevin woke up in a hospital bed with the worse headache he'd ever experienced. He could see Daria sitting next to him, hugging a lifejacket, with Jaclyn fast asleep in the chair next to her. A doctor was hovering over him.

"Welcome to the land of the living!" the doctor joked warmly. Kevin couldn't remember what had happened and the doctor explained that he received a concussion, probably from hitting his head when the boat heaved over a large wave. After examining him, the doctor left.

Daria stood up and moved closer to Kevin, still hugging the lifejacket. She explained how she was thrown overboard, and about Jaclyn's part in saving them both. She looked over at her still sleeping daughter.

"We're both okay." She looked down at the lifejacket. "Funny, but I can't seem to let this thing go. When Jaclyn threw it towards me, the wind picked up and carried it away from me. Then it started to move towards me...

against the wind and against the waves. Almost as if it were alive."

Kevin touched the lifejacket. He felt a sudden wave of love wash over him. He moved his hand over Daria's and they both held the lifejacket. A little hand reached up and touched the lifejacket as well.

"An angel lives in it!" Jaclyn said, making her parents chuckle. She looked at them. "Are you going to get a divorce?"

Kevin and Daria looked at each other, and both said, "No!" at the same time. Daria put the lifejacket aside as Kevin drew her and Jaclyn into a hug.

Epilogue

The writer stood inside the Pearly Gates. She was greeted by the two most important people she had lost during her life on Earth... her parents.

"Well, well, I hear you had to do a bit of time," her father said. "And as a lifejacket, of all things!"

"You were always such a handful as a child. And you lived a naughty adult life too." Her mother shook her head. "But why a lifejacket? You're a writer; couldn't you have gone back as a pen, or a book or something?"

The writer shrugged her shoulders. "I was looking for an easy way out. I figured a lifejacket would save a life and there I go... my job is done." She shook her head. "I saved a life, but it wasn't over. It seems I had to save a marriage too."

She linked arms with her parents. "Funny, but saving the marriage turned out to be the easy part. I guess the two of you taught me something after all."

St. Peter watched the trio as they made their way through the heavenly clouds. He smiled. "You did well, my writer friend, you did very well."

The Missing Fish

Jess stuck her head out the back door. "Okay guys, cookies are ready!"

Her husband Brent and their 8-year-old son Kevin dropped their rakes and quickly scrambled indoors, grateful for the break from raking leaves on such a cold November day.

"Woohoo!" shouted Kevin. "Chocolate chip cookies! My favourite!"

He sat down at the kitchen table, along with Brent and Jess. Two steaming cups of coffee and a cup of hot chocolate accompanied the home-made cookies. Every one quietly munched and drank while Jess, as was her habit, watched her fish swimming lazily around his fish bowl on the kitchen counter.

Only this time he wasn't swimming. Jess stood up and went to the counter, fearing that she may find her precious Siamese fighting fish floating fins-up on the surface of the water. She noticed the top of the fish bowl was clear of any dead bodies and felt a moment of relief. She moved around the bowl to see if the fish was tucked in behind the plastic plant. He wasn't there either. After a few moments of careful examination, Jess realized that the fish was nowhere in the bowl.

"Where's Ariel?" She looked at her family. They looked back at her.

"What do you mean?" Brent asked.

"Ariel," she replied. "He's not here!"

Brent got up to look at the bowl. "You're right. Where is he?"

"I don't know!" Jess began to look around on the kitchen counter and on the floor. "He couldn't have jumped out. His fins are too heavy. He's not that agile!"

"Maybe he is!" Brent looked down at the half-eaten cookie he was holding. "Um, how close were you to the fish bowl when you mixed the cookie dough?"

Jess looked at the plate of cookies on the table. "Ewww... Nah, that's impossible. Even if he did jump out, I would've notice a blue fish mixed in with a bunch of brown chocolate chips..." She looked at the plate of cookies again.

Brent patted her on the shoulder. "That's okay dear, I like seafood anyway."

"Oh don't be ridiculous! He's not in the cookies!" Jess turned to Kevin, who was quietly munching on a cookie. "Honey, when did you last see Ariel?"

Kevin gulped, and looked up. "Who, me? I dunno..." He quickly looked away.

"Honey, what's wrong?" Jess went back to the table. "Did something happen to Ariel? Don't worry about upsetting me, Kevin. I'm fond of him, but I realize that fish don't live for a long time."

Kevin burst into tears.

"Oh Sweetie, what's wrong?" Jess and Brent both went to hug him, but he pushed his parents' arms aside.

"You love that fish more than you love me," Kevin sobbed, "So I threw him out!"

Jess looked at Brent. Then she looked back at Kevin. "You threw Ariel out?"

Kevin sniffed. "Stupid name for a boy fish anyway... Ariel is a girl's name!"

"Well, not really," Brent explained. "You see, Ariel is a boy faerie in one of Shakespeare's plays..." Jess glared at him. "Ah, but that's not important..."

"What is important is that you have to realize that you are important, Kevin." Jess hugged her son. "I like having a fish around to look at. It relaxes me. But he's just a little critter that floats in water. You're our son, and the most important person in our lives."

She dried her son's eyes with a tissue. "Okay?"

"Okay," Kevin sniffed and blew his nose. "Sorry I threw Ariel down the sink."

Brent looked at him. "You didn't flush him down the toilet?"

Kevin shook his head. "When I pulled him out of the bowl, he got real skinny, so I just put him down the bathroom sink."

Brent looked at Jess. "He may still be stuck in the drainpipe. Let me get my tools!"

Several minutes later, Brent had the drainpipe opened up. He took the U-shaped pipe and turned it upside down in the plugged sink. A blue fish fell out, its gills still moving.

"He's alive!" Kevin shouted. Jess gently picked up her fish and brought him back into the kitchen, and back into his bowl. His fins spread out and he proceeded to swim lazily around his fish bowl on the kitchen counter.

Kevin looked at the fish and smiled. He turned to Jess. "Mom, can we go swimming?"

The Year of Firsts

It was all her fault. Nathan was only ten years old when his father died. Together they watched the cancer slowly take him, until the large, strong man they once knew became a thin, frail, dying man. When they placed the roses on his coffin and walked back hand in hand to the waiting limo, Nathan said, "When I grow up, I will find a cure for cancer." She smiled sadly at him. "Yes, you will."

And she believed it. The next day, she bought Nathan a chemistry kit. It was a simple starter kit, relatively safe. Together they watched magnesium burn. She remembered doing the same thing with her older brother when they were both children. The bright, white flame was mesmerizing, and she could tell Nathan was awed by it. Soon, he was calling water H_2O and salt sodium chloride. Her friends would chuckle, and his friends would simply be puzzled. He'd point to her bottle of Tums and say, "calcium carbonate". Trips to the library included science books. No Batman or Spiderman for him; Bill Nye the Science Guy was his hero.

All throughout school he aced his math and science classes. When he was a teenager, he turned the garage into a science lab. By then, his chemistry kits far exceeded burning magnesium. She was always worried that he'd mix the wrong chemicals and somehow hurt himself. "Don't worry, Mom," he'd say. "I know what I'm doing."

She'd smile and say, "Have you found that cure for cancer yet?" But Nathan always failed to see the humour in that, even after all these years. He would simply say, "I'm close." And she would encourage him and say, "Yes, I believe you are."

Then one day, two weeks after his 18th birthday, her nightmare happened. She was sitting in the living room watching television, when she felt herself being thrown across the room with a deafening explosion. And she knew. Ignoring the cuts and bruises, she quickly got up and ran outside. The garage was a wall of fire. She felt herself fall to her knees.

The next few days were a blur. Nathan's body, although miraculously intact, had suffered severe injuries and he had died instantly. Being a devout Catholic, she didn't fail to notice that he had died on All Souls Day, the day after Halloween. She hoped this was a good sign, and that he would be happy in Heaven with his father, with whom he was buried.

The following year was full of painful "firsts." The first Christmas without him was the worst. Even with all her friends and relatives rallying around her and keeping her busy, she still felt lost and alone. The first Easter was hard for her as well. She had always hidden eggs for him to hunt. Even as a teenager, he looked forward to it. She had videos of him, with his friends, with herself, always having fun. She couldn't bear to watch them.

And on top of all this, she felt guilty. Guilty for encouraging him to become a scientist. Guilty for buying him that first chemistry set, so that he could find that out-of-reach cure for a deadly disease.

She had the garage, or what was left of it, torn down and turned into a flower garden. She spent much of that first summer puttering in it. She thought she could feel his spirit in the flowers. "I'm sorry, Nathan." She would say. "It's all my fault."

The summer went by quickly, and the leaves were turning colour. Still, she would putter through the flower garden, now full of dying flowers, yet still full of bright reds and yellows from the falling maple leaves. The colours reminded her of the fire that almost a year ago took her son from her in this very spot. Just like the looming winter was taking the flowers. It should've saddened her, but she still felt her son's spirit in the garden, and it would always fill her will an odd sense of joy. She knew she was becoming obsessed with this, and thought she may need some grief counselling. She decided to wait until the year of "firsts" went by and then see how she felt.

Soon it was Halloween. It was a an unusually warm evening, so she decided to sit outside on the front porch, where she could still see the garden, and give out treats to the kids as they donned their scary little outfits and ran excitedly around the neighbourhood. She couldn't help but remember how Nathan would dress up as a spooky creature of some sort every year, first to go trick-or-treating, then later as a teenager to sit out on the porch and scare the kids with a "boo" or two before giving them their loot.

After the kids were long gone, and the street was once again quiet, she stayed sitting on the porch. She was dressed warm against the muggy, damp night, and soon fell asleep.

"Mom! Hey Mom!" She woke up with a start. How his voice sounded so real, she thought sadly. "Yo, Mom!" She looked at the garden and blinked. Nathan was sitting in the middle of the nearly dead flowers. "Don't be scared, Mom."

She smiled at him. "I'm not scared. I knew you were still here."

"Yeah, well, about that..." Nathan stood up, and she could see he was transparent, typically ghost-like. She got up and moved closer to him. She reached out to touch him, but her hand went right through him.

"Mom, I'm just here in spirit. You won't be able to touch me."

She fought back her tears and just nodded.

"Look Mom, I'm still here because I know you're having trouble letting go. I want to help you do that."

The tears spilled over her cheeks. "But it's all my fault!"

Nathan shook his head. "That's where you're wrong. You never forced me to like science. You only saw that it was what I wanted to do, and you encouraged me." He shrugged. "Frederick Banting discovered insulin, Alexander Fleming discovered penicillin. I bet their mothers wouldn't have felt guilty had something happen to them along the way. I almost discovered a cure for cancer. I was close. Don't feel guilty. Feel proud."

She smiled. "You were always such a brain." A thought dawned on her. "Is there some way I could pass on your work to someone who could finish what you started?"

"Now look who the brain is." But Nathan shook his head. "I can't give you anything. The cure is close, but the world isn't ready for it yet."

She sputtered. "But, but how can we not be ready to rid ourselves of such an awful disease?"

"I'm not sure of all the answers. Being dead doesn't give you all the answers. Personally, I think we all have to die from something. It would be great if we could cure all diseases, but then we'd have a severely overpopulated world. Just speaking scientifically, of course. Morally, I'd like nothing better than to make people live forever."

She nodded. "You always looked at the world through the eyes of science. I remember that one time I marvelled at the fact that we can save premature babies at such an early stage, and you simply said that we were weakening our species. Morally right, scientifically wrong. Yet we must do our best to save lives."

"And we do. We'll save even more as we move forward. Like I said, I was close. I'm sure someone else is just as close."

He looked around. "Pretty garden, Mom. But I won't be here much longer. It's time to say good-bye."

She wanted nothing more than to throw herself at Nathan's feet and beg him not to leave. But she knew he had to. He had to move on. And she needed closure, not grief counselling. She smiled through her tears. "Okay, then. Um, say hi to your dad for me, will you."

Nathan smiled. "Sure will. Bye." And he faded out.

"Bye Nathan," she whispered through fresh tears. She stood there for a few minutes longer, but she couldn't feel his spirit there any more. He was truly gone.

She slowly made her way back into the house. She noticed by the kitchen clock that it was well past midnight. All Souls Day. The year of "firsts" was over. And the rest of her life had begun.

What's That Smell?

"What's that smell?" Gary rubs his nose as his wife Paula and their daughter Chris breeze through the door. "Must be something outside. Hurry up and close the door!" With that he walks away.

Chris sniffs the air. "All I smell is your new perfume, Mom."

"He didn't even notice." Paula's lip starts to tremble. "All that work, and he didn't even notice." She bursts into tears and runs up the stairs to her room.

Gary strolls back into the hallway. "What's wrong with Mom?"

Chris rolls her eyes. "Gees, Dad, didn't you see her? She had a complete makeover done today. New clothes, new haircut, the works!" She shakes her head. "You know she's been feeling rotten lately, all worried about her age and everything. I convinced her to spend the day at a spa. Then we went to the mall. She was feeling great, until you spoiled it!"

She shakes her head again. "Honestly, men!" And with that, she runs up the stairs to her room.

Gary shakes his own head. "Honestly, women!" He climbs the stairs and goes to the bedroom he has happily shared with his wife for twenty-three years. Or so he thought it was happily shared. He quietly enters the room and sees Paula lying on the bed. Her hair is messed and her mascara is smudged from crying. She has taken off her new red sweater and black skirt and is now wearing her old sweat suit. But Gary, being more concerned with his wife's feelings, doesn't notice.

"Um, you look really great, dear," he stumbles through the compliment.

"Wahhh!" Paula bursts out crying again.

Chris comes into the room and looks at her dad. "What did you do now?"

"I just told her she looked great," he answers, a baffled look crossing his face.

Chris rolls her eyes again. "Good grief, Dad, look at her. She looks terrible!"

"You just told me she looked terrific!" He takes a good look at his sobbing wife. "Yikes, I guess she doesn't."

Chris looks from her mom to her dad. "Fix it!" she says and turns to leave.

He looks at Paula, whose eyes are now red and swollen from crying. Sheesh, he thinks to himself, how am I going to fix that? He unconsciously rubs an itch on his eyelid, taking care not to push his contact lens off centre.

Suddenly a thought hits him, and he suppresses a grin. He turns to Paula, who is wiping away her tears.

"Honey, since you got yourself a new outfit, why don't you put it back on and fix your makeup. I'll get dressed, and we'll go out for dinner. Oh, and I guess I'd better put my contact lenses in, so I can see what you look like."

Paula sniffs. "You mean you're not wearing them?"

Gary turns away. "No, um, I was just resting my eyes a bit when you came home."

"Oh, so you didn't see me when I came in?"

"Uh, not really, no."

Paula smiles. "Why don't you go to the bathroom and put them in then. In the meantime, I'll get dressed."

"Okay," Gary quickly leaves the room. He takes a deep breath, relieved that he managed to pull off that little white lie.

As she changes, Paula starts to chuckle. "You never were a good liar, my dear," she says under her breath. "But you meant well."

Gary washes up and decides to put on the new after-shave he just bought. After several minutes, he goes back to the bedroom to find his wife once again dressed and looking happy. "Wow, you look terrific! Give me a few minutes to get ready."

Paula smiles at him, and leans towards him to give him a kiss on the cheek. Suddenly, she stops short and wrinkles her nose.

"Ew," she says. "What's that smell?"

Love Affairs

———————————————

Crystals & Ice

Anthony Masoni watched his sister take her heavy gloves off and rub her hands for what seemed to be the hundredth time that evening.

"Crystal, why don't you go back to the house? It's freezing out here!"

Crystal laughed. "Of course it's freezing. That's why we're out here!" She slipped her gloves back on and continued pulling frozen grapes off the vine. "You know this may be the last time I can do this."

"Ah Sis, you've been saying that for the last ten years!" Anthony smiled at his beloved twin. "You're a regular diehard. Nothing's going to happen to you. But at least take a break. Go to the tent and have a warm drink."

Crystal smiled back at him. "Yeah, I could use some hot cider. But I'll be back soon!"

Anthony watched her slowly walk over to the heated tent. He had a dreadful feeling she was right this time. It may well be the last time she'd be able to work on the ice wine. She's been able to keep a brave front, but he could see the sickness in her face and in the slump of her shoulders. She didn't have a lot of time left.

His thoughts went back over the years. Their grandparents had come over from Italy, scrimped and saved the money they'd earned from working at a winery here in Southern Ontario, until they were able to buy some land of their own. They'd grown some grapes, made some wine, and quickly established "The Masoni Estate", a successful winery. Their only child, Anthony and Crystal's father, had continued the family business. He'd married their mother, and soon had the twins, who also continued the family business. Anthony and Crystal were only in their twenties when they lost both parents. Ironically, their mother had died from congestive heart disease while their father died two years later from a massive heart attack.

Anthony had been able to avoid the genetic disease. Crystal wasn't so lucky. Ten years ago, they had decided to try an ice wine line. The first icy cold day of the season was the day they were to pick the frozen grapes and quickly press them while they were frozen. That was also the first day Crystal had received the news... she had congestive heart disease. She'd kept it from Anthony until after their first ice wine was successfully bottled. He named the ice wine "Crystals & Ice".

His thoughts came back to the present as Crystal handed him a cup of cider. She looked around and spotted her two teenaged nephews working side by side. "I think your boys are going to do well with this business. At least I know it will be in good hands."

"Crystal," Anthony began.

"Let's not pretend, Anthony," she interrupted. "I was never lucky enough to marry and have a family. The Masoni Estate has been the love of my life." She sighed. "They've never been able to find a match for a heart transplant. I'm not well. I need to know that this place is going to be okay."

Anthony hugged her sister. "Could you at least not take your annual walk around the vineyard tonight?"

"Ah bro, you know that walk always clears my head after a hard night of grape-picking." She hugged him back. "If you don't mind, I think I'll take that walk right now."

"Sure thing. But make it a short one; you need your rest."

Crystal smiled at him and walked away. He had an ominous feeling that he'd just seen her smile for the last time.

Crystal went back to the tent and picked up her backpack. She pulled out flashlight and headed towards the back of the vineyard and into the copse. She looked around to make sure nobody was following her. Nobody ever did. She found her usual spot, the spot she sat down at ten years ago and cried at the news of her failing health. She pulled out her blanket, spread it out; she then pulled out her bottle of ice wine and two glasses. She waited.

Gabriel first came to her when she had been crying all those years ago. A handsome stranger, a fairy tale prince; he took her in his arms and soothed her. Normally, she would have bolted if any man would have done this, but he brought a sense of peace and happiness to her that night. And warmth. She should've been frozen when she went back to the house, but all she had felt was the warmth.

The next year, after picking the frozen grapes, she went back to the copse, this time with one of the first bottles of Crystals & Ice that they had produced the prior season. Gabriel showed up again. They drank the wine and made love in the warmth of the copse on a bitterly cold night. The next morning, she woke up in the warm copse and found the bottle of wine was still full.

She went back on every first cold night of the year, after she finished picking the frozen grapes.

And this night, like the past ten years, Gabriel showed up. They drank wine and made love. They lay in each other's arms.

"Tonight, the wine will be gone," Gabriel told her.

She looked at him. "Then I will be going with you?"

"Yes."

She looked back towards the house.

"Don't worry about your family," he told her. "They will take care of the business." He lifted his glass and drank. "They will do your memory great justice."

Crystal smiled and stood. "Then I am ready to go."

Gabriel took her hand. Together they walked through the copse and into the endless warmth of a beautiful summer day.

The next day, when Crystal failed to show up at the breakfast table, Anthony knew. He put his coat on and walked to the back of the vineyard and into the copse. There he found his sister in her eternal sleep, with a glow in her cheeks and a smile on her face. There was an empty bottle of Crystals & Ice in the crook of her arm.

"Oh my dear sister, you died holding the love of your life, didn't you?" He wiped the tears from his eyes and picked her up. "Well, at least I got to see you smile one more time." He carried her back to the house.

Cupid and the Mortal Heart

"Cupid, you must sit and take some nourishment!" Apollo watched his friend nervously pacing and running his fingers through his golden curls. "You have a long day ahead of you." He held out a goblet. "At least have some merlot. Bacchus makes the best!"

"Of course he does!" Cupid retorted. "He's the god of wine!" He sighed and took the goblet from Apollo. "All the gods are good at something. Except me. Every Valentine's Day, I visit the planet Earth and fling arrows of love around. But do the mortals love one another? No, all they do is fight!" He shook his head. "I'm such a screw-up."

Apollo knitted his eyebrows. "What is a screw-up? Oh, it does not matter. It seems that your visits to Earth have given you a unique dialect." He chuckled. "Nobody understands you."

Cupid ignored him. "Why was I chosen to be the symbol of Valentine's Day? Why couldn't my mother Venus do it?"

Apollo smiled. "Ah yes, your mother is, how would you say it? One hot mama!"

Cupid cringed. "For the love of gravy, Apollo, that's my mother! You're sick!"

"I do not feel ill, my friend. And what is this 'gravy' we are to love?"

"Never mind. Janus and Ceres will soon be here to transport me to Earth." Cupid finished his merlot. "I think I'll stay away from Hollywood this year. I really messed up there. I can't believe I accidentally shot Angelina with the arrow that was meant for Jennifer. I was really hoping to patch things up between her and Brad..."

Apollo smiled again. "What you need is a little romance for yourself. Whatever happened to that lovely Greek goddess that stole your heart?"

"You mean Chaos? Zeus sent her to Earth, well, to create a little chaos." Cupid rolled his eyes. "Apparently, he was bored and needed some amusement. Well, he's certainly getting it. I hear he's been getting some laughs over some government battle in a place they call Canada. Guess I'd better pack some extra arrows for them."

Apollo looked up as Janus and Ceres entered the room. "Ah, there you both are. Would you care to join us for some merlot before you send our little friend off to the mortal world?" He poured two more glasses. "It seems our Cupid is a little reluctant to go. He is losing perspective of his task."

Ceres nodded. "I have noticed that Cupid has been disgruntled lately." She turned to him. "Young Cupid, perhaps you need to understand the mortal heart in order to help it. Would you be willing to spend some time as a mortal?"

Cupid's eyes widened. "You can do that for me?"

Ceres chuckled. "Well, I am goddess of the Earth. However, I can only grant you mortal form for three days."

Cupid laughed. "Well then, bring it on, baby!"

Ceres blinked. "Excuse me?"

"What I mean is, yes, I would like to be a mortal. Thank you, Ceres."

Ceres raised her hand and waved it over Cupid. A small cloud surrounded him for a few moments and then dissipated. Blue jeans and a denim jacket replaced his toga.

Apollo choked on his merlot. "What on Earth is he wearing?"

Ceres laughed. "You have answered your own question, Apollo. He is wearing what is on Earth." She turned back to Cupid and handed him an odd-looking bag. "This is a backpack. I have replaced your large bow with a smaller crossbow. Mortals prefer their weapons to be concealed, so you must be careful not to let anybody see you using it. Remember, as a mortal, you will be seen."

"Will anybody recognize me, do you think?"

"Hardly. Mortals think Cupid is a cherub, not a full-grown man. Oh, and another thing... You cannot walk through walls. And do not drink wine while on Earth. Bacchus does not make it, so it can make you quite intoxicated if you are not used to it."

"Okay, got it!" Cupid turned to Janus. "Alright, god-of-doors-dude, open up that portal to good old Planet Earth for me, would you!"

Janus swung his arm in a circular motion and opened up a large hole in the air. "There you go, my friend. The best of luck to you."

"Thanks Janus. You da man!"

Apollo, Janus and Ceres watched Cupid walk through the hole.

Janus turned to the other two. "What is a Yu-da Man?"

* * * *

Cupid spent the next couple of days wandering the streets of a very busy place he recognized as New York City. He usually enjoyed his work there. It was densely populated, and this gave him much-needed target practice. He chuckled to himself. New Yorkers love to love, thanks to him. So far, he had no need to take out his crossbow. But then, he couldn't go through any walls to be able to salvage any love spats amongst sweethearts.

There were many couples out for a walk through Central Park on this unusually warm February day, and Cupid spent most of his time observing them. He was glad to see that mortals had similar courtship rituals to those of gods and goddesses. And he filled with pride as he realized that his arrows of love had a lot to do with it. True, he could never solve the problems of the world, but at least he was able to bring to it what love he could, especially on Valentine's Day.

His thoughts were interrupted by loud voices. He turned to see a young couple sitting on a park bench, arguing. Without thinking, he pulled out his crossbow and aimed it at them. He then heard some screaming behind him.

"Look out! He's got a weapon!" "It's a gun!" "No, it's a crossbow!" "Someone call the cops!"

Suddenly, he felt the weight of several bodies fall on top of him. He then felt himself being dragged up on his feet. The crossbow in his hand disintegrated as several men pinned him flat against a tree. Moments later, two strangely robed men he recognized as law enforcers bound his hands with metal cuffs.

"You have the right to remain silent..." Cupid was too confused speak, so he decided to take the law enforcer's advice. He was place in a vehicle and taken to jail.

Before being place in a cell, a detective sat him down and began questioning him.

"What's your name?" he asked.

"Cupid."

"Oh great, a nut case!" The detective rolled his eyes. "And I supposed you live on Mount Olympus."

"Oh no,' Cupid replied. "The Greek gods live there. I'm a Roman god."

"Sure you are," the detective continued. "How old are you?"

"Two thousand, one hundred and forty-three," Cupid smiled. "I'm one of the younger gods."

"Listen, you nut case, you're in serious trouble! What did you do with the crossbow?"

"Apollo probably took it back. He keeps my bows and arrows with his own when I'm not using them."

The detective sighed and stood up. "Okay, you're going to sit in a cell until we can straighten this out."

Cupid spent the rest of the day in a cell with two other men. They looked dangerous, but he found that they enjoyed his stories about his ventures as the god of love. Like the detective, they also called him "Nutcase".

Later on that evening, the two men were taken away, and he had the cell to himself. He noticed that his mortal form felt fatigued, so decided to lie down and have a nap.

He was soon awakened by a clanking sound. He looked up to see a pretty brunette opening the cell door. "Okay Cupid, come with me."

He followed her out into the main area, where he noticed the law enforcers were all fast asleep at their desks. She led him out the door and into the street. Soon they disappeared into the bustle of the city's nightlife.

"Where are we going?" Cupid asked her. "And why didn't you call me by my mortal name?'

"Which is?'

"Nutcase."

The brunette laughed. "Because I know you are not a nut case." She led him into a quiet Greek café. "Nicolas, bring some wine for my friend here."

Cupid shook his head. "Oh no, I can't have any wine."

The woman smiled. "You can have this one." Nicolas poured two glasses and left the bottle on the table for them.

Cupid looked at the label. It read, "Bacchus Merlot". He looked up at the woman. She just smiled. He shook his head. "Now, I'm really confused."

"I will explain later. In the meantime, let us spend the evening enjoying the city as young couples do."

"Oh, um, that would be lovely," Cupid stammered. "But my heart belongs to Chaos."

The woman chuckled. "Everybody's heart belongs to chaos." She stared at him. "Look into my eyes."

Cupid stared at her. She was beginning to look familiar. Soon her features changed and Cupid gasped. "Chaos, it's you!"

"Yes, my love," she laughed.

He got out of his chair and pulled her up out of hers. He lifted her into a hug and spun her around. "My gods, it's been too long!"

"Only three hundred years," she said. "But it felt like millenniums!"

Cupid put her back down. "I came here in mortal form to study the mortal heart. I am happy to see that it beats just as strongly as a god's heart. Especially where love is concerned."

Chaos smiled. "Well then, we have one more day left before you go home. Are you willing to explore our mortal hearts a little further?"

Cupid laughed and hugged her again. "In a heartbeat, baby... in a heartbeat!"

Double Trouble

I stood nervously next to Mark and glanced around the room. It had been twenty-five years since I'd seen most of these people, and I began to wonder why I wanted to come to this high school reunion in the first place. Even though Mark went to the same school and knew the same people, he didn't seem as eager as I was to see them all again.

Mark nudged me. "There's Annie." I felt a wave of relief as my best friend came towards us.

"Hi guys!" She gave us both a hug and a peck on the cheek. "Oh good, you're both wearing your hello-my-name-is stickers." She smiled and winked. "Not that we need them. The three of us haven't changed a bit."

I looked at Mark's full, but prematurely white head of hair, then self-consciously ran my fingers through my own bottled brunette locks. I laughed nervously. "No, not a bit."

"I saved your seats at that far table over there," Annie pointed towards the corner. She swung around to leave. "I'll see you over there in a few minutes, after we mingle a bit." She stopped in her tracks, looked at me and winked. "Oh, by the way, both the Marconi twins are here... Double Trouble." She chuckled and walked away.

I gasped. Double Trouble. I had totally forgotten that nickname. It was given to me while I was dating Robbie, one of the twins. He and Sam were so identical, even their own mother had trouble distinguishing who was who. Apparently one of them had a birthmark on his butt. Neither twin would ever say which one of them had it.

As I made my way around the room greeting old friends and classmates, I looked around for Robbie's shock of long, wavy black hair. Then I realized that I may have to look for short gray hair, if any hair at all. I then wondered if he still had that lithe athletic body, or whether he married a fine cook who managed to fatten him up a bit. Or a lot. After a few minutes I spotted a handsome man with a lithe athletic body and wavy black, but a lot shorter, hair.

Without a second thought, I walked over to him. "Robbie?"

He hesitated a moment, then smiled. "Lorrie?" He then laughed and gave me a bear hug. "Wow, you haven't changed a bit!"

"Neither have you! Still the same sweet, shy fella I knew, right?"

"Oh, you never knew me that well, did you? I was the loud, arrogant twin. Still am." He laughed. "And I bet you'd still get me confused with my brother. Right bro?"

"Lorrie!" Again I was swept up in a bear hug, this time by Sam. At least, I thought it was Sam. He looked just as good as his brother. And still just as identical. Now I was confused.

I turned back to Robbie. "I never got you mixed up with Sam."

Both twins burst out laughing. Robbie said, "Honey, I am Sam!"

I looked at Sam, who apparently was now Robbie. "Well, it's been twenty-five years. But back then, I never got you mixed up with Sam."

Sam chuckled. "It wouldn't have mattered anyway, since you were dating both of us."

I stared at him. "What? No I didn't. I never dated you."

Sam's smile faded. "Gee, I was hoping our dates were a little more memorable. Don't you remember that picnic by the waterfall?"

My jaw dropped open. I looked at Robbie. "But that was with you!"

Robbie shook his head. "No it wasn't."

Sam continued. "And that time we went skating?"

"But you were on the hockey team. You wouldn't have wobbled and fallen all over the place." I looked at Robbie. "You were the one who couldn't skate!"

Sam chuckled. "That was me. You kept calling me Robbie, so I just played along and pretended to skate like Robbie would have. I thought you were joking too."

I shook my head in disbelief. Then I felt myself pale. "Uh, exactly which one of you took me out to Princess Point to make out?"

They both broke out laughing. Robbie said, "Maybe you should've checked out the butt to see if it had a birthmark!"

Our conversation, and my revelation, ended there as other classmates came over to greet the twins and myself. After a few minutes, I numbly walked over to Annie, who standing against the wall and scanning the room.

"Annie, which twin did I date?"

"Huh?"

"Which Marconi twin did I date?"

"Lorrie, don't be silly. You dated both of them." She chuckled. "Why do you think everyone called you Double Trouble?"

I shook my head. "Everyone knew I was dating both twins?"

"Well of course! You can't keep something like that quiet in high school."

"Okay... right." I looked around for Mark. He was chatting with some people. I went over to him. He saw the bewildered look on my face and excused himself. He took me outside for some fresh air.

"Are you okay?" He smiled. "I hope those Marconi twins didn't try to pull your heart strings again. If I didn't know they were both happily married, I'd be mighty jealous."

"Mark, you and I didn't really date until the end of our final year. But can you remember which Marconi twin I dated prior to that?"

"Now you're really trying to make me jealous." He pretended to look hurt. "You dated both of them. Everyone knew that."

I threw my hands up. "Everyone except me!"

I spent the rest of my night going over my high school relationship with what appeared to be two-boys-in-one. To this day, I still don't know which twin was which, or what I did with each, or both, of them. All I know is that they were, and always will be, double trouble.

The Best Years

Catherine sits on a bench outside the luxurious hotel, suitcase at her side, and watches her friend Audrey as she flirts with a pleasant-looking older man. The fact that his wife is standing next to him doesn't stop Audrey. Although she never married, Audrey has always been comfortable around men. Even at the age of 50, the blonde bombshell still turns heads. They have been the best of friends since childhood, but Catherine has always felt frumpy next to her, even though she inherited her mother's classic Italian beauty and still turns heads herself.

The tour bus that was to take them to the dock wasn't due for a good half hour. Catherine leans back on the bench and thinks back to the reason she is taking this cruise. It is hard to believe that a year has gone by since her husband left her. That unforgettable conversation seemed to have taken place just yesterday.

Steve had been cool towards her for several weeks. He avoided her affections, constantly claiming that he was tired from all the work the law firm was piling on him. His eight-hour days became twelve-hour days. They never went out together anymore. It didn't take long for Catherine to suspect that he was having an affair. She decided to confront him.

"Okay, this is enough," she said to him one evening. "Steve, if there is someone else, we need to talk about it."

Steve looked at her in shock. He then shook his head and sat down on the couch. "I should have known you'd suspect something. I just wanted to be sure about things before I talked to you."

He sighed and rubbed his face with both hands. "You're right, Catherine. I'm afraid I fell in love with someone else."

Even though she knew all along, his admittance still made her numb. She slowly sunk down on the couch next to him. "My God."

"My God, indeed," Steve replied. "I'm so sorry. I just don't know what to say."

Catherine blinked. "You said you're in love with someone else. Are you telling me this isn't just some middle-age thing you're going through?"

"Oh honey, I wish I could. I've always loved you so much. I still do. This just happened to me; I wasn't looking for an extra-marital affair."

They sat quietly for a few minutes, lost in their own thoughts. Suddenly Catherine let out a nervous laugh. "Well, at least I know it's not your secretary. Oops, I mean associate. Joseph doesn't like it when people call him a secretary."

Steve went pale. His mouth opened as if to say something, but then closed again.

"Steve, are you alright? What's wrong? Did something happen to Joseph?" Catherine looked at him. Suddenly, she knew.

"Oh my God!" she shrieked. "Joseph? Are you telling me you're gay? Twenty-five years of marriage and it was all a lie?"

"No, it was not all a lie!" Steve took a deep breath and slowly let it out. "I loved you all those years and never questioned my sexuality. I didn't fall in love with Joseph because he was a man. I fell in love with Joseph because he was Joseph."

Steve covered his face with his hands. Then he looked up at Catherine. "He didn't consider himself gay either. It was just something that happened between us."

Catherine nodded. "Okay, your sexuality isn't the issue here, then. The fact is that our marriage is over. Now we have to tell our two daughters that you're leaving me for another man."

"They're adults, and fortunately, very liberal-minded. I'm sure they'll be angry at first, but they will learn to accept it." Steve got up from the couch.

"I'm so sorry, Catherine!" He slowly headed towards the stairs. "I'll pack my things."

Catherine sat frozen on the couch while Steve packed his belongings. She sat frozen while he went out the door, loaded the trunk of his car and drove off. She sat frozen throughout half the night. Then she got up, went to the bathroom and threw up.

Now, Catherine is sitting frozen on the bench as the tour bus pulls up. Audrey shakes her shoulder and breaks her trance.

"Earth to Catherine," she says. "Bus is here."

They gather their luggage and line up to board the bus.

"Where were you just now?" Audrey asks her.

"You don't want to know," Catherine replies, then changes the subject. "I'm a little nervous about this singles' thing."

"Honey, you need this. You haven't dated since your divorce." Audrey chuckles. "Think of yourself as a born-again virgin."

"Why did you talk me into this?" Catherine looks around at the other people boarding the bus. "What makes me worry is the small print in the cruise's flyer. You know, the one that says 'Clothing Optional'."

Audrey roars with laughter. "Take a look at these folks. They're all middle-aged. That caption should read 'Clothing Preferable'!"

She sees the look of doubt on Catherine's face. "Aw honey, don't worry. It's a singles' cruise, not a swingers' cruise. No one is going to expect you to drop your drawers or anything. Although it might not be a bad idea."

"Easy for you to say, you've been dropping your drawers all your life!"

Audrey gives her an incredulous look. "I beg your pardon?"

"You know what I mean. You've been single all your life. You've had a variety of drawer-dropping. Me, I've had twenty-five years of the same thing."

"Then it's time you start sampling some new, uh, things. Anyway, you'll just see the odd bare-breasted sunbather. That's all it means."

"Well, at least it's an older crowd. I guess that's why this is called 'The Best Years Cruise'. Not that it's been my best year." Catherine sighs.

Audrey looks at the crowd gathered near the bus. "I expect there will be several buses for this crowd. We might as well take our time."

They spend the next half hour chatting with the other people who are waiting for the buses to arrive. They pleasantly smile through the Hepburn jokes, something they've had to deal with throughout their lives because of their names, even though Catherine spells her name with a C. The warm Florida sun feels good this early in the morning and the tourists anticipate the cruise around the

Bermuda coast, with stops at Hamilton, King's Warf and St. George.

Catherine finds herself standing next to a handsome man approximately her age. He looks at her with warm brown eyes and smiles. She notes how his salt and peppered hair adds to his good looks and silently curses the fact that she has to rely on a bottle to keep her own hair dark and youthful. He introduces himself as David, and when she offers her hand to shake, he holds it for a moment longer, causing her to blush.

"You're newly divorced, aren't you?" he asks her. Her blush deepens.

"I don't mean to embarrass you. You just look very uncomfortable." David smiles again. "I know how you feel. I'm newly divorced myself."

He shakes his head. "My wife left me for another woman."

Catherine looks at him for a moment, then begins to chuckle. David looks hurt.

"I'm sorry, it isn't funny, but to quote you, I know how you feel!"

David looks at her and smiles. "Why, did your wife run off with another woman?"

Catherine laughs again, and David joins in. "I don't think I want to know the answer to that. Oh well, looks like it's time to load up a bus or two. See you aboard!"

"You sure will!" she calls after him as he heads for the bus. She joins Audrey in line. "This may not be so painful after all. Heck, maybe by the end of the week I'll have the nerve to sunbathe topless."

Audrey looks at her. "Well, don't expect me to apply aloe gel to your sunburn!"

They reach the door of the bus. "Well," Audrey turns to Catherine. "Are you ready to start enjoying the best years of your life?"

Catherine smiles at her. "Yes, I am!" She looks around behind her and sees the older gentleman that Audrey was flirting with earlier in line further down behind them.

She points him out to Audrey. "Say, doesn't that guy have a wife?"

"Nah, that was his sister. She just came by to say 'bon voyage'." Audrey giggles. "He's really charming. I promised him an on-board date."

Catherine giggles along with her friend. "Maybe he's rich!"

"Hey, at our age, money isn't important!" Audrey lowers her voice. "What's important is that they can still, ahem, you know..."

They both burst out laughing as they board the bus, once again turning heads.

The Decision

The mist in the crystal ball swirled, mixing the blue and red streaks of colour until it became a pale purple. Alex leaned back and enjoyed the light show, while at the same time admiring Lucia, the pretty fortune-teller leaning over the ball. He'd expected her to be typically dolled up in gypsy clothes with wild black hair and even wilder made-up eyes. Instead, this pony-tailed brunette was simply clad in blue jeans and a Paxton Winter Fair t-shirt. Her blue eyes weren't wild, but he imagined they could be during a passionate moment.

He chided himself as he remembered that Julie was just outside the booth, waiting for him to come out with great news about his future. Of course, he didn't believe in fortune telling, but since they were at the fair, he might as well have some fun with it.

"Oh." The gasp was barely a whisper, but it caught Alex's attention. He looked at Lucia, who was wearing a surprised expression. She quickly donned a blank expression.

"What is it?" Alex asked.

Lucia carefully kept her face blank while staring into the crystal ball. "Don't worry, it's nothing bad. But you will have a very important decision to make by the end of the day." She looked at Alex. "Take your time, and follow your heart."

Alex looked into her eyes. Oh yes, he thought, her eyes definitely do go wild with passion. When she remained silent, he said, "That's it?"

Lucia smiled. "That's all you'll have time for today."

Alex left the booth and joined Julie, who was looking around the busy indoor pavilion. "Oh there you are," she said. "I see a coffee stand down that way. Let's grab one and then we can discuss our fortunes."

As they headed towards the stand, Alex said, 'Not much to tell. I'm supposed to be making an important decision today."

They reached the coffee stand. The aroma of several flavoured coffees mingled in the air. Alex chuckled. "Maybe I'd better do some serious thinking here. I wouldn't want to get French Vanilla, if indeed my future depends on Irish Cream."

Julie raised an eyebrow. "Alex, I know you don't believe in psychics, but you know I do. And Lucia came highly recommended. She's not a fake. If she says you have a decision to make, then you do!"

Alex sighed. "Irish Cream it is, then."

Julie ignored him and they purchased their coffees. They sat in the lounge area and relaxed for a few minutes before continuing their stroll through the fair.

"Funny, but Lucia told me a similar thing. She said that something was going to happen today that would change my future as well." Julie looked at Alex. "I wonder if all this has something to do with us."

"Well, it is Valentine's Day today. Maybe I'm supposed to propose to you or something."

"Alex, please be serious!"

"I am serious! We've never really discussed our future." Alex looked at Julie and smiled. "Maybe today is the day we should."

Julie shook her head. "Honestly Alex, you know I don't want to get married. I'm too busy with my practice. I see sick children all day, and much as I love them all, I don't want any of my own."

Alex sighed. He and Julie had been dating for a couple of years, and being a doctor himself, he understood the hectic pace of owning a practice. He respected Julie's decisions about her future, but couldn't understand them. Busy professionals married and raised families successfully all the time. His thoughts went back to Lucia. Heck, busy clairvoyants probably did too!

They spent the rest of the afternoon taking in the fair. They rode the indoor amusement rides and watched the outdoor husky sled races. But Alex's mind kept wandering back to the decision he was supposed to make. He couldn't understand why it was even on his mind. He didn't believe in psychics, but somehow Lucia left quite an impression on him. In more ways than one, he realized.

He noticed Julie was quiet as well. Figuring she might be a little tired, he suggested they go for dinner. She agreed, so they headed for a cosy restaurant nearby.

They both sat quietly while eating their meals. In an effort to break the mood, Alex held up his wine glass and said, "Happy Valentine's Day, Julie."

Julie chuckled. "Silly! You know I'm not sentimental about Valentine's Day." But she brought her glass up to his anyway. They both took a sip and put their glasses down.

Julie's smile disappeared. "Alex, maybe we should talk about our future."

Alex nodded. "I think so too."

Julie continued. "The truth is, I don't think we have one."

Alex's eyes widened. "Oh?"

Julie hurried on. "Oh, I'm crazy about you, Alex, and we've had a great couple of years together." She shook her head. "But we don't want the same things."

Alex nodded again. He didn't say anything, but he felt a strange sense of relief.

"I'm sorry, Alex."

"Yeah, so am I." He held up his glass. "Well, Happy Valentine's Day anyway."

Julie laughed, somewhat relieved as well. "Okay, Happy Valentine's Day!" They clinked glasses again.

After dinner, they walked back to the fairgrounds, where Julie left her car. They talked about their relationship and decided they could part amicably enough to be able to stay in touch, at least professionally. Julie got into her car and drove away.

Alex stood in the parking lot next to his own car, but he didn't feel like going home yet. There was something he felt he had to do in order to complete his decision. He headed back towards the pavilion.

The fair was still going strong, but teenagers and young adults now replaced the families and couples. Alex went straight to Lucia's booth and peaked around the partition. Lucia, her back turned towards him, was straightening up a few things.

"You came back," she said, without turning around.

"Um, yes," he said sheepishly, and came into the booth. "I decided to take your advice and follow my heart."

Lucia turned around and smiled at him. "So you did."

Just then, her crystal ball glowed a bright red and then faded quickly.

Alex looked at Lucia. "How did you do that?"

"You did that," she answered. She looked at Alex with wild blue eyes. "I think my ball is trying to tell us something."

Alex felt as if his heart was dancing. "I decided to come back and see if you'd like to perhaps spend the rest of the evening with me."

"Now that," she said, "was a good decision."

The Green Valentine

I was taking off my gloves when the phone rang. Without taking off my boots, I ran across the kitchen to answer it. I didn't want to; I knew it would be Jim and I knew he wouldn't be coming home.

"Hi Babe, it's me," he said. "I'm sorry, but I just can't get a flight home. Everything flying into Southern Ontario is cancelled."

I looked out the window. I was never a lover of snow, but I didn't recall ever hating it as much as I did at that moment. "I didn't think you'd be coming home any time soon. It's been snowing for two days straight. I was just out there shovelling for the umpteenth time."

"I wish I could be there." Jim sounded sad.

I thought of him looking out of his hotel window at the green palm trees and the blue ocean. At the beautiful women in thong bikinis. I felt a pang of jealousy. "No you don't!" I said, a bit too sharply. He remained silent. I calmed down. "I know you're there on business, but trust me, you're better off there. At least your scenery is green. I wish mine was."

"I know," he said softly. "Happy Valentine's Day."

"Happy Valentine's Day, Honey." I answered.

I hung up the phone and sat down to take my boots off. I rubbed my frozen toes for a few moments, then got up to take my coat and hat off. I walked across the kitchen in my stocking feet and felt the cold wet snow I tracked in seep into my socks. I thought of the palm trees in Jeff's part of the world and started to cry.

Later that day, I prepared myself to go out for more shovelling. As I was putting on my coat, I looked out the window at the snow-covered street. I noticed a pizza delivery truck struggling to get through the drifts. I wondered who would've ordered take-out, and who was actually delivering in the blizzard. The truck reached the front of my house and pulled into my poorly shovelled driveway. I went to the door and opened it.

"I didn't order pizza," I called out to the young man as he stepped out of truck. He just smiled and reached into the back seat. He pulled out a large pizza box and brought it up to me.

"I was told to deliver this to you." He handed me the box and returned to his truck.

I brought the box into the kitchen, thinking that perhaps Jim ordered it for me. He knew pizza was my comfort food. I noticed the box wasn't warm and there was no heavenly cheesy fragrance coming from it. I opened it.

It was filled with luscious green palm leaves, and in the middle sat a small box with a note. I opened the box first. It contained a beautiful emerald pendant surrounded by small diamonds on a white gold chain. I opened the note. It said, "I know how much white makes you blue, so I sent you some green. Happy Valentine's Day."

I started to cry again.

The Green Valentine – Part II

Jim stares out the window at the raging snowstorm. He knows he should be out there shovelling. Normally, he would go out to shovel every couple of hours, just to stay on top of it. But today isn't a normal day. Today is Valentine's Day. And he would be spending it alone.

Once again, he picks up the pizza box and opens it. The small jewellery box is still there, nestled among the withered palm leaves. He picks up the note that's tucked between the leaves. "I know how much white makes you blue, so I sent you some green. Happy Valentine's Day."

Was it only a year ago that he had it sent to her? He closes his eyes as he recalls sitting in the warmth of the Jamaican sun that day. His flight home had been cancelled because of a snowstorm pummelling all of Ontario, similar to the one outside his window now. He had thought about his petite wife braving the elements and shovelling the snow with the strength of an athlete. He then called his friend Dean, a jeweller, who had set up the pizza delivery.

He smiles sadly as he recalls his wife telling him that she had honestly thought he was sending her a pizza. Instead she opened the pizza box to find an emerald necklace nestled in luscious green palm leaves. Palm leaves that have now withered. Just like his wife had withered. And he didn't even realize she had withered, until it was too late.

She always hated the winter season. The short days made her tired, the snow made her irritable. And it didn't help that he had to travel for business. He would've loved to take her with him, but it wasn't feasible. So she would spend days at a time alone, yet she never complained.

But he noticed the change in her when he finally got home from that trip last year. She seemed quiet. Whenever he asked what was wrong, she would simply reply, "Nothing." She would accept his caresses, but he could feel the lack of passion when he held her in his arms. He tried to let it pass for a while; spring was just around the corner, and he figured she would snap out of it.

But as the days got longer and warmer, she just got quieter and colder. He noticed that she never wore the emerald necklace, but simply kept it in the pizza box inside her closet. He would to try to talk to her about her sadness, but she insisted that nothing was wrong.

Then came the day he was to leave for another business trip. He was reluctant to go. He didn't want to leave her, but she again insisted that she was fine, and would probably spend the next couple of days working in the garden. So he went on his trip. He called her as often as possible, and she always reassured him that she was fine.

When he called her on the morning he was to fly home, there was no answer. She hadn't answered her cell phone either. He figured she probably just forgot to take it with her. But he felt that there was something wrong. He was relieved when he finally boarded his plane to come home.

He arrived home later that evening. It was already dark, yet there were no lights on. The car was in the driveway. He felt uneasy; she wasn't one to go to bed early, and besides, she knew he was coming home that night. She had always waited up for him in the past.

He unlocked the door and went inside, calling her name. He turned the light on in the living room, and found her fast asleep on the couch. Except he knew she wasn't asleep. Oh, she wasn't tragically draped across the couch, pillbox in hand and pills strewn across the room. She was simply lying there, the way she normally would when she took a catnap. But he knew she was gone. She had a peaceful smile on her face, one he hadn't seen in a long time.

Now he picks up the jewellery box. Ever since she died, he has never been able to bring himself to open the box. He knows he has to do so eventually. Why not today? It's Valentine's Day and this was, after all, the very last Valentine's gift her ever gave her.

He opens the box. A small, folded piece a paper falls out. He stares at the emerald, daintily surrounded by tiny diamonds. He puts the box down, picks up the piece of paper and unfolds it. It's a note in her handwriting. "White has always made me blue, but not even this beautiful green will take away the blackness that I crave."

He begins to cry.

The Intruder

"I'm glad you called," I turned away from the phone to stifle a yawn. "Can't wait 'til you come home tomorrow." I failed to stifle the next yawn.

John laughed. "You'd better get some sleep. Hug the dog for me. And stay safe."

It was my turn to laugh. I always did when I thought of my big husband scooping up our little Chihuahua for a cuddle. It was nice to have my two guys around, but that night I only had Diablo to take care of me. I looked down at him, already curled up and asleep on my bed.

I smiled into the phone. "Don't worry, Diablo will protect me, all eight pounds of him."

We said our good-byes and hung up. I slipped out of my housecoat and under the covers. Diablo woke up and crawled under the sheets with me. "Good guard dog!" I mumbled and shortly fell asleep.

I woke up to the sound of somebody fumbling with the keys at the front door. The door opened, then closed. "John's home," I thought to myself, and dozed off again. Then something inside jolted me awake, and in moments I was sitting up. I realized that it couldn't be John; he was on the other side of the continent for a business meeting. Nor could it be our son since he and his wife lived an hour away from here and wouldn't show up this late unannounced. Or would they? Did something happen?

I turned on the side table light, jumped out of bed and put my housecoat on. I looked back at the bed and noticed the little lump of covers that contained Diablo, still fast asleep. "Yeah, great guard dog!" I whispered at the lump. I headed toward the door, and stopped in my tracks. It suddenly occurred to me that what I heard downstairs might be an intruder. I felt a lump in the pit of my stomach and swallowed my panic. I looked around for a weapon but couldn't see anything pliable. I picked up my spray perfume bottle and hoped that I didn't have to mace anybody with Obsession.

I headed back out the door, only to become startled by the fierce yapping of my trusty guard dog. Diablo jumped off the bed and raced downstairs. "Well great, so much for the element of surprise," I whispered through clenched teeth. I continued to creep towards the staircase, all the while listening carefully for any growling or barking, or for human threats to my dog. All was quiet. I prayed that Diablo wasn't hurt. I took the steps slowly and quietly, successfully avoiding the creaks in the last two. With perfume bottle ready in my hand, I crept along the wall until I reached the living room. I peaked around the edge.

Diablo was standing on the arm of the couch, his tail wagging furiously. He was looking down at a human form that seemed to be flailed across the couch, fast asleep. Thankful for the full moon's light shining into the window, I was able to make out the man's features. And it was a man. The one who lived next door.

I felt a great wave of relief wash over me as I realized what had happened. We lived in a semi-attached house; Evan and his wife Rachel lived in the other half of the semi. Our two front doors were next to each other. Since we were good friends as well as neighbours, we had entrusted each other with our house keys. I wondered why Evan would let himself into the wrong door. Upon closer inspection, the reek of alcohol answered my question.

I turned on the light and leaned over to shake him. "Evan!" I spoke quietly and got no response. I shook him harder and yelled, "Evan, wake up!"

"Whaaa..." Evan jumped quickly to his feet, knocking me off balance. I fell against him, and together we fell onto the couch. We struggled in confusion, all the while the both of us grunting and shouting. Diablo, not wanting to miss out on play time, jumped on us and began barking. I could feel my silky housecoat and nightgown slip up around my waist, and tried to pull it down. This caused us to topple onto the ground. I screamed. Evan screamed. Then somebody else screamed.

We managed to detangle ourselves and both looked up to see Rachel standing over us, fury written all over her face.

"I can't believe this!" She fumed. "I knew Evan was fooling around on me, but I would've never suspected you!"

"What?" Evan and I chimed together. I noticed my nightgown was still riding high around my waist and quickly pulled it down as I got up. I looked over at Evan, and was relieved to see he was too busy dragging himself up on the couch to notice.

I looked at Rachel and felt myself blush under her hard stare. "Um, it's not how it looks?" I thought about the absurdity of the situation and stifled a nervous giggle.

Rachel looked at Evan, who was now sitting on the couch with Diablo curled up on his lap. She burst into tears. Evan got up from the couch and stumbled over to her. "Now honey, stop this! I'm not cheating on you."

"Yes you are," she sniffled and pointed at me. "With her!"

"Don't be ridiculous! If I was going to cheat on you, it wouldn't be with her!"

"Huh?" I blinked. "What's wrong with me?"

Evan flushed. "No no, there's nothing wrong with you..."

Rachel burst into fresh tears.

I sighed. "Look, let's just all sit down and figure this out."

I took the easy chair, while Evan and Rachel sat on the couch. Diablo took his place back on Evan's lap. Evan looked around. "Ah, why are we here?" I explained how he must've let himself into the wrong house.

He rubbed his head. "Right. Me and the guys had a little too much to drink, I guess." He smiled. "The Leafs won, by the way."

That piqued my interest. "Really? You think maybe they'll make the playoffs this year?"

"Ahem!"

"Sorry Rachel," I said. "Now, why do you think Evan is cheating on you?"

She sniffed. "He hasn't touched me in weeks!"

I groaned inwardly. Oh no, not one of those he-hasn't-touched-me-in-weeks problems, I thought to myself.

"Aw honey, it's not that I don't want to, it's just... just..." Evan began to stutter. He always stuttered when he was embarrassed, and I got the feeling that I really didn't want to hear this.

"W-well," he continued. "I'm just having a little problem with..."

"Okay, why don't I just leave you two alone," I quickly suggested as I stood up.

Evan looked at me and blushed. "Oh no, it's not that!"

I sat back down again. Now I was curious.

He cleared his throat and turned back to Rachel. "Like I was saying, I'm having a little problem with you. Well, not you yourself, but... W-well, it's your housecoat."

"My housecoat?" Rachel looked down at the ratty old blue fleece material she was wrapped in. "What's wrong with my housecoat?"

"Well, frankly, I hate it. You've had it since we've been married. That's over thirty years! And lately, when you wear it at bedtime, it just turns me off."

Rachel just stared at him. "Oh."

Evan looked at me. I felt his stare glaze up and down and I knew he was going to give Rachel the why-can't-you-be-more-like-her line. I decided to save this marriage before it hit rock bottom.

"Rachel, let's try something," I stood up and reached for her hand, pulling her up from the couch. "We're the same size. Let's trade housecoats for a minute."

She looked uncertain. "Well, okay." We both removed our housecoats. I was pleased to see that she was wearing a pretty pink negligee. I noticed Evan's eyes widening as he stared at her. So far so good, I thought. I handed her my silky red housecoat and she put it on.

"Now go look in the hall mirror," I said. She disappeared for a moment. I smiled at Evan, and thought I detected a grateful look.

Rachel came back into the living room wearing a big grin. "Wow, I look great. Thank you so much; you're a good friend." She gave me a hug. "Oh, and I found this." She held up my bottle of Obsession, which I must've dropped during my struggle with Evan. She sprayed some on herself and handed me the bottle. She then grabbed Evan's hand, pulled him off the couch, out of the living room, and out the front door.

"Um, my housecoat?" I said to the empty room. Diablo just stood in the middle of the room wagging his tail. I put on Rachel's housecoat. It was warm and cosy, and I understood why she kept it for all those years.

I locked front door and headed back upstairs to the bedroom, vaguely wondering whether my new housecoat would mark disaster for my own healthy marriage.

The Island

"Enjoy your day on the island. Please be on deck by 5 p.m. so that we may sail back to shore in time for the evening."

The tinny voice clicked off and everybody filed into line to exit the small ferry. Samantha and Valerie picked up their bags and joined the crowd.

"I can't wait to soak up the sunshine!" Samantha squealed.

The two men lined up in front of them both turned and looked the voluptuous bleach-blonde ladies up and down. "We can't wait either," one of them said and they both snickered.

"Hnh!" Valerie rolled her eyes. "Honestly, men!"

It was Samantha's turn to snicker. "If only they knew," she whispered to Valerie. Valerie smiled back. They got off the ferry and hurried away from the leering men.

They walked along the beach for several minutes until they found a nice area surrounded by a large copse of palm trees near a quaint bar. They sat at a table and took a few moments to look around.

Samantha sighed. "Now what?"

"I don't know, Samantha. This is my first time at a nude beach too, you know."

Samantha looked at Valerie. "Are you having second thoughts about this?"

Valerie shook her head. "Not really. But we may have a problem. How do we go from being Samantha and Valerie to being Sam and Val? The change rooms aren't exactly private. If we go into the ladies' rooms, we'll be coming out as men. And we can't go into the men's rooms while we're ladies."

"Shh!" Samantha hissed, as the two men from the ferry came up to the table.

"May we join you?" one of them asked.

Samantha stuttered. "Well-"

Valerie cut her off. "Yes, please do!" She gave her baffled friend a wink.

The two men, who were still wearing their swimming trunks, sat down. They introduced themselves as Eric and Nathan.

"So why aren't you ladies dressing down yet?" Eric asked.

"Oh, we will be," Valerie said. She stood up. "Why don't you gentlemen get us some margaritas while Samantha and I go to the change rooms?"

The two men agreed. Valerie and Samantha headed towards the change rooms.

"What are you up to, Valerie?" Samantha asked.

"I'll explain while we're in the cubicles."

"You mean the one in the ladies' rooms?" Samantha gasped.

"You bet!" Valerie laughed as they entered the change rooms.

Ten minutes later, several screams came from the ladies' rooms as two naked men wearing blonde wigs raced out. They quickly ran through the palm trees and up behind the table where the two men were waiting for Samantha and Valerie. With lightning speed, the naked men took the wigs from their heads and placed them onto the heads of the two unaware men sitting at the table sipping margaritas.

"There they are!" a panicky female voice yelled. Through the trees, Sam and Val could see two security guards pulling the bewildered and bewigged Eric and Nathan up from the table and taking them away.

Sam laughed. "Well, that was certainly the most unusual way we've ever gotten out of drag."

Val chuckled as they calmly made their way back to the nude beach.

"Um, Val?"

"Yeah?"

"How are we going to turn ourselves back into Samantha and Valerie?"

"Hmm... I never thought that far ahead. We may have to be men for a while."

Sam shrugged. "That's okay. These are, after all, our birthday suits. We might as well show them off."

The two friends laughed as they settled down to soak up the sunshine.

Under the Rose Garden

Martha stood in the rose garden, the spade in her gloved hand dangling at her side. She felt a moment of sadness, like she did this time of year, every year. Preparing the garden for the oncoming winter always reminded her of another summer gone, and another year of her life gone with it. She looked towards the cornfields, where Joe was doing some last minute preparations and sighed. Farming was a lot of work, especially for Martha since she was born and raised in the city, but she liked the fresh air and solitude.

And she wasn't always happy here. Joe and Martha's marriage saw its share of bumpy roads. First she found out she wasn't able to have children, and then there was Joe's infidelity. Those hurdles were overcome, and they'd been happy for the last twenty years. But now she's been dealing with a bout of depression, just one of the many ups and downs of her menopausal roller coaster ride. Oh, she'd tried everything from hormone therapy to Prozac. Only one thing worked. She absently slipped her free hand into her pocket and clutched the small prescription bottle.

Then her mind went blank. Again. She stared at the rose bushes she'd just cut back and was mounding with soil. Think... think... Oh yes, two more bushes to go. She hated it when she blanked out like that. Dang this getting older anyway! She got down on her knees and began to mound the next bush.

She loved her rose garden. Joe had surprised her with it all those years ago, when they'd reconciled their marriage. She had been staying with her mother while she and Joe went for counselling. Yes, Joe had cheated on her, but he wasn't a womanizer, and she'd decided that he had turned to another woman because she herself was wallowing in self-pity and shutting him out. She felt she'd let him down by not being able to have children. But they both fought to keep their marriage alive, and she had come back home to a beautiful garden.

As she shifted around the bush, she felt herself sink into the soil. Oh yes, she'd meant to tell Joe about that. She noticed that the ground had been shifting a bit around the garden ever since the bad rainstorm that had flooded it last spring. She had lost a few of the bushes, but fortunately, the cornfields had drained well.

She stayed on her hands and knees and crawled back a bit. Then she noticed a bright red sparkle near the rose bush. She reached out and poked at it with her spade. It looked like a ring. She picked it up and gasped. It was a beautiful ruby ring! She glanced back and noticed something else. A small stick. No, it was a chicken bone. Or was it? She picked it up. Perhaps some animal found the ring and ingested it, just to meet its fate under her rose garden? She glanced at the bush again and noticed a couple more bones slightly protruding out of the soil. She lightly dusted the dirt off the bones, until she revealed what looked like a human hand. She felt a chill go down her spine and she screamed. Then her mind went blank, and everything went black.

Martha felt something cool on her face. She opened her eyes, and saw Joe leaning over her with a washcloth in his hands.

He smiled at her. "Welcome back!"

Martha knitted her brows in confusion. Why was she lying in bed? Then she remembered her grim discovery and sat up. She gave a small cry, and Joe gently took her in his arms.

"Take it easy, honey," he spoke soothingly as he held her. "It's all taken care of. While you were passed out, I called the police and then I called Dr. Wallace."

He let go of her, and leaned over to pick up her pill bottle. "Dr. Wallace wanted me to give you a couple of these as soon as you woke up." He handed her two pills and held out a glass of water for her.

"B-but," she stuttered. "Wh-what about the body? Who is that?"

"I asked the authorities to remove it right away. I knew it would upset you. The police cordoned off your rose garden until they can investigate." He held out the glass. "Now, please take those pills. You need to rest until you get over the shock."

Martha looked at the pills in her hands. Valium. It didn't cure her depression, but the muscle relaxant certainly made her, well, relax. She knew two pills would easily knock her out. She thought about the body buried under her rose garden, and decided she wanted to sleep for as long as she could. She took the pills.

She spent the next couple of days in and out of consciousness as Joe fed her a diet of toast, tea and Valium. She knew she'd have to face the demons eventually, but still she welcomed the escape. On her wobbly trips to the bathroom, she'd look out the window, where she could see her rose garden. It was cordoned off with yellow tape, just as Joe said, but she could also see that the dirt had been moved and some of the bushes were missing. She didn't care; she'd never be able to work that garden again.

On the third day, she decided to forgo the pills. She knew she couldn't sleep forever. She asked Joe to help her downstairs and out to the garden.

"Are you sure?" Joe asked.

Martha nodded. "The police will want to question me eventually anyway. I have to face this."

Joe sighed. "Well, okay, but I don't think the police will bother you. I told them you weren't well."

"That's fine, but I still need to face this." She got out of bed and put her housecoat on. She made her way downstairs on shaky legs with Joe at her side. Together they walked out to the garden. She could now see the yellow caution tape and the disturbed soil.

"Who was that?" Martha asked Joe. "And how did she get under my garden?"

Joe shrugged. "I don't know. She certainly wasn't there when I put the garden in. She must've been buried deep and somehow was worked up during that rainstorm we had." He took Martha's arm. "Come on back to the house, now. I don't want you to have a relapse."

He led her back upstairs and into bed, where he coaxed her to take her pills. As she began to doze off, she realized that there was something amiss about the crime scene, but in her subconscious state, couldn't put her finger on it.

Later that night, she was able to sit up and eat some supper. Her head had cleared a bit, and she began to ponder what it was that was bothering her about the garden. When Joe handed her two more pills, she slipped them under her tongue rather than argue with him. When he left to sleep in the guest room so as not to disturb her rest, she spit the pills out and thought some more. But she fell asleep anyway.

She woke up the next morning in a startled state. Her mind was as clear as a bell, and she realized what was bothering her. The caution tape! The police doesn't use caution tape; they use the same yellow tape, but with the words "Police line; do not cross" on it!

When Joe came in, she mentioned it to him. He simply smiled and told her that they probably just ran out of the proper tape. When she asked him if there was any further news on the body, he said there wasn't, and handed her two more pills. Once again, she placed them under her tongue. Joe then left to work the fields.

Martha appreciated how Joe was trying to protect her, but she needed to know what was happening, so she called the local police station. She spoke with the desk sergeant, who informed her that her husband had never called with a report of a body under a rose garden. Martha felt that familiar chill in her spine again. She hung up the phone. She felt her mind going blank, but fought it. She went down to the cornfields.

She felt both fear and fury as she walked up to Joe. "Why didn't you report the body? Who was she?"

Joe sighed. He took Martha's hand and led her back towards the house. "I was hoping you'd never find out."

"Find out what?"

"She was the woman I had an affair with."

Martha felt herself going faint, but once again fought it. "You killed her?"

Joe nodded. "Yes." He led a shocked Martha to the patio swing, and they sat down. "You see, she became pregnant. She wanted me to leave you so we could have the baby together. Well, by then you and I were getting our relationship back together, and I told her that I would take responsibility as the father of her baby, but you were never to know about it, because I knew it would devastate you, with your not being able to have children." He shook his head. "She just went nuts on me. Started hitting me and kicking me. I just pushed her away, but she lost her balance, fell and hit her head. She died instantly. I panicked. She was new in town, and I knew she had no family, so I just brought her back to the farm and buried her. Then I decided to plant a rose garden before you came home, in case you wondered about the disturbed soil."

Martha sat perfectly still. Her mind blanked out, but she could see a police cruiser coming up the lane. Why was it here? Oh yes, the phone call she made. "Where is the body now?" She asked quietly.

"Still under the rose garden." Joe watched the cruiser as well. "I guess I won't be stopping to smell the roses any more." He stood up, caressed Martha across her cheek, and made his way to meet the cruiser, and his fate.

Wine and Roses

Lily nervously sipped on her glass of red wine and stared at the doorway, waiting for the man who would be carrying a bouquet of roses. She'd seen the photo he sent her, so she had an idea of what to look for: a fairly handsome, middle-aged man with gray hair and a goatee. She ran her fingers through her own bottled brunette locks and sighed at the unfairness of only men being allowed to age gracefully.

Her thoughts were interrupted by the sight of a dozen red roses coming through the door, followed by the familiar face. He looked around momentarily, then locked eyes with Lily and smiled.

"Lily!" He came to her table and took her hand. "You're photo doesn't do you justice. You are gorgeous!" He handed her the roses.

Lily blushed. "Thank you, Nate, they're beautiful. But you didn't need to bring them. I recognized you right away. Have a seat."

Nate sat down and then picked up the bottle of wine. "I see you started without me." He refilled her half-empty glass and poured himself one.

"Sorry, I just got a little nervous."

"If it makes you feel better, I was a bit nervous myself." Nate smiled. "Silly, isn't it, considering we've been chatting online for a couple years now."

"True." Lily relaxed a bit and looked around the room. "This is a pretty place, isn't it? And the name is so appropriate!"

"Wine and Roses!" Nate chuckled. "This winery has been in my family for three generations. It was my idea to set up a restaurant here."

Lily sipped her wine. "This red wine is fabulous! I don't usually like the local reds."

"Thank you!" Nate looked at her. "Isn't it an amazing coincidence that your online name is Roses and mine is Wine? What are the chances!"

"And considering my name is Lily, yet I went with another flower." Lily picked up the bouquet and brought them to her nose. "Mmm, I do love roses!"

"And I love wine!" Nate caught the odd look Lily gave him and stammered. "Er, I mean the business as well as the wine itself. Don't worry, I'm not a lush or anything!"

Lily laughed. "I didn't think you were."

They spent a few minutes perusing the menu and giving their orders to the attentive waiter. He refilled their wine glasses and took the orders to the kitchen.

"I guess dinner will be perfect for the boss man," Lily grinned.

Nate laughed. "I expect dinner to be perfect for all my patrons!"

"I'm so glad I had to fly out here for this convention," Lily said. "Selling insurance isn't the most exciting job in the world, but at least it allows me to see a bit of the world."

"Well, I'm glad it finally brought you to my town!"

They lapsed into some small talk until their food came, then lapsed into total silence while they ate their delicious meal. They continued their conversation over glasses of ice wine.

Lily giggled. "I'm so glad you didn't turn out to be an axe murderer."

Nate choked on a mouthful of wine. He bellowed out a hearty laugh. "And here I thought you were the axe murderer!"

"L-O-L," Lily spelled out, and they both laughed again.

Lily looked at her watch and sighed. "I have to get going. I've got an early meeting in the morning."

They both stood up. Lily picked up her roses and they made their way out of the restaurant and into the warm spring night, where they waited for Lily's taxi.

Nate smiled at her. "So, what do you think?"

"You mean, about us?"

He nodded. "Is there an 'us'?"

Lily looked at him. "I think there's been an 'us' for a long time now. Unfortunately, there are two provinces between 'us'."

Nate sighed. "The closer we get, the further away we seem to be."

A taxicab pulled into the parking lot and headed towards them. They turned to each other and instinctively leaned into each other to share a kiss.

"See you, Roses!"

"See you, Wine!"

Lily got into the cab and looked out the window at Nate. He waved as the cab pulled away, leaving them both to wonder if there would be any kind of future for 'us'.

'T is The Season

The Doubting Pumpkin

The day started out cool and wet, but soon the sun was out to dry the leaves that blew throughout the pumpkin patch. Jesse rolled back and forth, shaking off the leaves that had covered him throughout the morning. He looked up and down the long vine and noticed his siblings were doing the same thing.

Sammy, the largest pumpkin on the vine, whooped with glee. "Today's the day, kids! We're getting harvested and sold to the market. Before you know it, we'll be glowing Jack-O-Lanterns!"

Little Lucy giggled. "I hope my new owner puts a pink hat on me."

"I hope mine carves me up to look real mean! Grrrr!" growled Terry.

Jesse noticed all the other vine families in the patch laughing and chattering with excitement as well. He didn't understand why everybody was so happy. He turned to Sammy. "I don't get it. We're going to get cut up! Our insides are going to be used for pumpkin pie, and they'll roast our seeds!"

Sammy laughed. "Not all our seeds, Jesse! The farmer will be keeping some of us so that he can reseed the patch." He looked at the worried expression on Jesse's face. "Aw, come on Jesse, you remember what our mother told us while we were still seedlings inside of her."

"Yeah, I know. She said that whatever we get used for, it'll be totally painless, and our spirit will still live on." He sighed. "Maybe she just said that so we wouldn't be scared."

147

"If that were true and we really in some sort of trouble, wouldn't she have rolled away from here to save us? And don't forget when the farmer cut her open and took us out, she didn't cry out. She just said good-bye to us, and that was it."

"Yeah, I guess." But Jesse wasn't convinced. He noticed the farmer and his helpers had begun picking pumpkins from the other vines. Pumpkins were calling out their good-byes as they were picked off the vine and placed onto the backs of several trucks.

Soon it was Sammy's turn to be picked. He turned to Jesse. "Remember what I told ya, kid. Don't sweat it." The helper picked him up. "Later!" Sammy waved to his siblings and disappeared into the back of a truck. Jesse was still waving back when he felt a pair of hands lift him. He felt the vine gently separate from his head and he was placed into the back of another truck. Well, so far so good, he thought.

He heard a familiar giggle and turned around to see Lucy and Terry sitting beside him. "Isn't this exciting?" Lucy said.

"Yeah, a real hoot," Jesse answered sarcastically. The back of the truck was closed, and he gasped.

Terry laughed. "You're such a doubting pumpkin, Jesse."

Jesse ignored him and nervously settled back for the long ride to the market.

Three days later, Jesse, Terry and Lucy were relaxing on the straw bedding of the market stall, along with the other unsold pumpkins. Jesse began to wonder what would become of them if they weren't sold soon. Ripped open for pumpkin seeds, no doubt, he thought.

Just then, a little girl ran up to the stall, followed by her mom. "Oh look, Mommy!" she pointed towards Jesse's direction. "These three pumpkins look the same! Maybe they're brothers and sisters!"

Her mommy laughed. "Maybe they are. Shall we bring them home and carve them?"

The little girl and her mommy picked up Jesse, Terry and Lucy, and placed them into their shopping buggy. Jesse began to panic. "No!" he cried out. "Please don't hurt us!"

"Jesse, don't be silly," Lucy said. "People can't hear us! They can't even see us! They just see our outer shells."

"And they won't hurt us!" Terry added. "Honestly Jesse, we'll be fine."

A few hours later, the three pumpkins were placed on the front porch of the little girl's house.

"When are they going to carve us, I wonder?" Jesse said.

"Probably not until Halloween next week," Lucy answered. "For now, we're just going to decorate the front porch the way we are."

"I can't stand this," Jesse said. "I'm going to run away." He began to move back and forth, trying to pick up enough momentum to roll away.

"Jesse, don't!" Terry yelled. "You'll smash if you roll down those steps!"

Terry moved towards Jesse to try to block him, but Jesse had already begun to roll and he bumped into Terry, who ended up falling down the steps himself. He bumped down the four cement steps and landed on the bottom with a splat. He cracked in half and fell open.

Lucy gasped. "Oh no!"

Jesse stared at his brother, or rather at his two pieces of brother. "What have I done?"

The little girl ran outside and down the steps. "Mommy!" she called out. "One of the pumpkins broke!"

Her mom came outside and picked up the pieces of Terry. "That's okay, dear. We'll just use this one for pie, and then I'll roast the seeds." She brought Terry into the house.

The little girl looked at the other two pumpkins. "Don't worry, we'll take care of your brother," she told them and went back into the house.

Lucy and Jesse looked at each other in shock.

"Do you think...?"

"How did she know?"

They looked towards the door and then back at each other again. "Nah!" They said at the same time.

The morning Jesse had dreaded finally arrived. It was still dark outside when the little girl came out, patted both pumpkins on the head and said, "We get to carve you today! I can't wait." She went back inside the house.

"Oh no." Jesse began to cry.

"Aw Jesse, it'll be okay." Lucy tried to console him, but Jesse continued to cry. Suddenly, there was a flash of light at the bottom of the steps and she turned towards it. She gasped. "Jesse, look!"

Jesse sniffed and looked towards the light. "Oh my!"

There at the bottom of the steps were three of the most beautifully carved pumpkins he had ever seen. One of them had a happy face with pretty eyes, and the other two were carved to look mean and scary, yet they weren't really scary at all. All three were glowing brilliantly.

The happy face stepped forward. "Hello Jesse and Lucy. I'm you mother."

The two scary faces laughed. "I bet you can't tell who we are!" one of them said.

Jesse recognized Sammy's voice. "You're Sammy!" He turned to the other scary face. "Then you must be Terry! And Mom, am I ever glad to see you!"

Lucy looked at Terry. "Oh, but how did you become a Jack-O-Lantern, Terry? You became a pie pumpkin when you broke."

"We all become Jack-O-Lanterns, no matter what happens to us!" Terry replied.

Mom spoke. "That's right, children. Remember I told you that our spirits live on. People can't see us, but we're always around to make Halloween a fun and happy time." She turned to Jesse. "So you see, my little doubting pumpkin, there is nothing to be afraid of."

Jesse felt a surge of relief wash through him. He nodded to him mom. "You're right, Mom. I see now that I have nothing to worry about."

Just then, other pumpkins began showing up. Jesse recognized them as his other siblings from the vine at the farm. They were all wearing various faces, and some were even wearing hats.

Lucy giggled. "I hope the little girl puts a pink hat on me!"

Just then the door opened and the little girl stepped out. She bent down in front of Lucy. "Look at what I have for you." She placed a pink hat on Lucy's head, and went back inside the house.

151

Lucy and Jesse looked at each other in shock.

"Do you think...?"

"How did she know?"

They looked towards the door and then back at each other again. "Nah!" They said at the same time and everybody laughed.

The Missing Ingredient

In the deepest, darkest corner of the woods, where even the trees are afraid to grow, there is a small clearing. At the edge of this clearing sits a terrified dog. Once every year, and always on All Hallows Eve (and unbeknownst to the poor dog) a small, hunched figure of a man prowls the area, searching, searching.

The mysterious figure has only begun this year's search. He stops his prowling when he sees the lost Golden Retriever shivering in the moonlight. He smiles at his good fortune, for he normally has a full evening's hunt in this neck of the woods. He slowly approaches the animal.

"Hello, fella. You look a little lost!" His soft-spoken manner seems to calm the dog. The man gets down on his haunches, and allows the animal to sniff his hand. "That's right, I won't hurt you. But I do need a little something from you."

The dog looks up at the man's face. The moon is shining directly on it, exposing a collection of warts across its cheeks and nose. Not sensing any danger, the dog stands perfectly still as the man clips several locks of hair from his tail.

The man pats the dog on the head and gets up to leave. "Thank you, fella, that's all I needed." He begins to walk away, and then turns around to look at the dog. "Um, you are a fella, aren't you? Dang, I forgot to check!" He shrugs his shoulders. "Oh, well, dog hair is dog hair!" and continues his journey back home. Within an hour, he is back in the Master's cave, and he proudly hands over the dog hair.

"Well done Luna. And fast too!" The Master takes the hair and brings it over to a boiling cauldron. "Maybe this year we will be lucky." He catches a glimpse of his reflection in the mirror and shivers. "I can't believe I've been toad-faced for a whole year!"

Luna shrugs his shoulders. "Master, every year it's the same thing. You have a recipe to make you so handsome that the ladies will fall into your arms. The only problem is, you're missing an ingredient. And all you know about this ingredient is that you must find it on All Hallows Eve, and you must concoct and take the potion on the same night." He huffs in frustration. "You've been doing this for two hundred and forty-seven years. You've turned yourself into everything from a hummingbird to an elephant!" He snickers. "Obviously, the toad's spit you used last year didn't work either."

"I know, I know!" the Master sighs. "Quit nagging me, Luna. It was my grandfather's recipe, and being the jokester that he was, he left out that one ingredient. You know, once we figure it out, this potion can work for you too."

"No thank you Master." Luna proudly looks at himself in the mirror. "The ladies like me just the way I am. They seem to find my inner beauty!"

The Master looks at Luna's wart collection. "Yeesh, you'd need a bucket of salicylic acid to find your inner beauty!" He turns back to the cauldron. "Well, here goes!" he says, and throws the dog hair into the mixture. He stirs it, then takes a ladle and dips it in. He takes a drink.

The cave begins to shake. Then the thunder and lightning (which is mandatory to every horror story) puts in its appearance. The Master then becomes engulfed in the proverbial puff of smoke. The smoke clears, and once again he is transformed into a new person.

"How do I look?" he anxiously asks his assistant, not yet wanting to look in the mirror.

Luna's eyes bulge. The he smiles. "Oh, just fine, Master. Absolutely wonderful!"

"Really?" The Master begins a self-frisk. He sees that his hair, which he always kept long, has thickened into luxurious golden curls. He touches his face. Soft and dainty. Same with his hands. "Something's not right here..." He looks down inside his now oversized black robe and screams.

"EEK! I'm a girl!" He looks in the mirror and sees the most beautiful blond woman he has ever laid his eyes on. "Wow, I'm gorgeous!" Again, he panics. "And I sound like Michael Jackson!"

Luna chuckles. "No, more like his sister Janet!"

The Master looks at him. "Ah, Luna, did you happen to check the dog to see it if was a male?"

Luna gulps. "Uh, no, I, uh, kinda forgot. It looked like a male dog. You know, those Golden Retrievers are kinda hairy. Can't really see their parts. Heh heh..." He gulps again.

"You bumbling fool!" he yells. He looks back at Luna and sighs. Then he looks down his robe again. "Hey, I've got a couple of nice hooters in here!"

"Can I see?" Luna creeps up to him and reaches out to touch the Master's breast. The Master slaps his hand away.

"Don't get fresh!" He looks down at his wizard's robe. "Is the mall open at this time of night? I really need some new clothes. If I'm going to be a woman for a year, I may as well enjoy it."

"Mind if I enjoy it too?" Luna is beginning to drool.

The Master rolls his eyes. Then he begins to look around.

"What are you looking for?" Luna asks him.

"My purse. If I'm going to the mall, I need my purse! Oh heck, I don't have one."

"You can always buy one at the mall," Luna suggests.

"How can I go shopping for a purse if I don't have a purse to shop with? Oh, never mind, let's go!"

They leave the cave. "Well, at least we're on the right track," says the Master. "Next year, you'll have to get me a lock of Brad Pitt's hair."

"Good idea, Master!" replies Luna. He smiles as he begins to plan a way to get a lock of Angelina Jolie's hair for next year's ingredient.

Harry's Toothache

Harry Wolfe had a toothache. He'd had it for several days now. It had started to ache after he ate that silly cat he'd been stalking. It was well fed and slow on its feet, an easy target for Harry. So when full moon arrived, he had decided to feast on it. Heck, how was he to know the dang thing had swallowed a stone? He broke his favourite fang on it when he pounced on the cat.

Now it was aching like a son-of-a-gun. And he wasn't sure what to do about it. He'd already tried to visit a couple of dentists, but he had frightened everybody off when he entered their offices. So he stole the Novocain and went home. The Novocain helped a bit, but now he only had a bit left. He sighed. "Life sucks," he thought to himself. "Too bad I get to live forever."

"Harry!"

He cringed at Elvira's voice. "Yes, dear?"

"Are you going to do something about that tooth?" She stood in the doorway, hands on her ample hips. "Go see a dentist, or something!"

"I've tried, but I keep scaring them off!" Harry scratched his furry face. "This may be a handsome face to you, but it scares the crap out of mortals!"

Elvira rolled her eyes. She turned around and left the room, all the while mumbling something about how she should've married Wolfman Jack when he proposed to her all those years ago.

Harry shook his head. He wondered why he stayed with her. True, she had the wildest black hair and the reddest three-inch nails this side of the realm. And her figure; well, he was certainly grateful that she would never age. "Oh here I go thinking with the wrong werewolf part again," he muttered to himself.

Elvira re-entered the room. "I have a good idea. Tomorrow is Halloween. Why don't I try to make a dentist appointment for tomorrow? Everyone will think we're in costumes, so nobody will get scared when we show up."

"Elvira, that's a great idea!" Harry tried to smile, but winced from the pain. "I knew I married you for something."

"Harry, you married me because I have big ta-tas," she fired back. "So don't go thinking you love me for my mind!" She turned around and left the room again. Harry snickered and drank down the last of his Novocain.

The next day, Harry and Elvira climbed into their pink and white '55 Buick. Harry slumped down in the passenger seat, while Elvira proudly drove her beloved vehicle into town.

"Why can't we get a new car?" Harry groaned. "I swear we get the weirdest looks in this thing."

"Nonsense," Elvira smiled and waved at a group of high school kids standing at the corner. "Everybody is just jealous. I mean, look at us! Here we are, a handsome couple in a vintage car to die for!"

Harry chuckled. "Well, it won't be us doing the dying, will it!"

Elvira laughed. "I just wish this car could last as long as we will. Hey, maybe we can start going to those vintage car meets. We don't get out much. It would be nice to make some new friends."

"Aw now honeybunch, we've tried that. We're always scaring everybody off, and what few friends we do make get old and die. It's so heart-breaking."

Elvira sighed. "You're right. I guess we'll just have to stick to visiting the other realm during the full moon." She glared at Harry. "Whenever you're not off chasing cats, that is."

"I can't help it, dear," Harry shrugged his shoulders. "I just get the urge during the full moon. Hey, at least I don't feast on people any more. Yuck, they're so polluted these days!"

Elvira snorted. "Hah, you think their pets are any better? I swear Harry, some day you're going to eat the wrong critter."

"Well, it's not like I'll die from it, or anything! As long as I don't ingest any silver bullets, I should be alright." He looked at her. "And besides, look at all the fur coats you've been able to make with my leftovers."

Elvira patted Harry's hand. "True. Although I get funny looks when I wear my Dalmatian coat, like I'm that witch from the Disney movie or something."

A few minutes later, they pulled into a parking spot. As they got out of their car, a man waved at them. "Nice costumes!"

"See?" Elvira said to Harry. "We shouldn't have any problems today."

They heard a wolf whistle. They turned around to find a small crew of construction workers ogling Elvira. She giggled. She heard a "hmph" come from Harry and turned to him. "Jealous?"

He hmphed again. "Those guys've got nothin' on me." He possessively put his arm around Elvira and they continued down the street, enjoying the attention their supposed costumes were attracting. They reached the dentist's office and stepped inside.

The receptionist looked up and smiled. She was dressed in black and wearing a witch's hat. She offered a cheery, "Hello!" Her eyes went back and forth between Harry and Elvira. "Wow, those costumes are awesome!"

"Thank you," Elvira said. "I'm Mrs. Wolfe. I spoke to you yesterday about my husband's tooth."

"Of course. Please take a seat. Dr. Stoker will be with you shortly." The receptionist pointed a black-tipped finger towards the waiting room.

"Oh my," Elvira mused. "Who does your nails?" The receptionist chuckled.

As they sat in the waiting room, Harry perused Dr. Stoker's Diploma in Dentistry that was hanging on the wall. "Interesting name. I wonder if he's a descendant of that fellow who wrote about Count Dracula."

"Who knows," Elvira replied. "The Count always gets a good chuckle out of that book. It made him quite famous in the mortal world."

"Well, the Count doesn't drink human blood any more. Hasn't touched the stuff in decades." Harry sighed. "I swear, with the way this world is going, we're all going to end up becoming vegetarians. And where's the satisfaction of a good hunt there? Imagine me, pouncing on carrots!"

Elvira patted his knee. "Don't worry, dear, I'm sure I can come up with some tasty brews in my cauldron if comes to that."

"Mr. Wolfe, the dentist will see you now." Harry followed the receptionist into one of the rooms, while Elvira stayed in the waiting room, reading an old copy of Hunter's Digest.

Harry sat fidgeting in the dentist chair. He'd always been healthy, and this was his first visit to any kind of medical practitioner. Oh, he'd been to countless warlocks for checkups over the centuries, but that was just for peace of mind, seeing that he was immortal. He looked at the dentist's tools that were neatly laid out next to him and cringed.

Just then a tall man dressed as a clown came in, followed by a young women dressed in a skimpy French maid outfit. "Hello, I'm Dr. Stoker," he introduced himself, "and this is Pamela, my assistant. Happy Halloween!" He chuckled. "Now, what can we do for you?"

Harry tore his gaze away from Pamela and looked at the dentist. "I broke my fang on a cat," he explained.

Dr. Stoker looked at him. "A cat?"

"Well, it was actually on a stone that was in the cat."

Dr. Stoker and Pamela looked at each other.

Harry continued. "You see, I got a little hungry one night and, well, I ate this cat. Only he ate a stone. So when I bit into him, I broke my fang on the stone."

Dr. Stoker and Pamela looked at each other again.

"Hmm, you ate a cat that ate a stone," Dr. Stoker mumbled and rubbed his chin. "Okay Mr. Wolfe, why don't you just lay back on the chair and we'll have a look." He adjusted the chair and Harry felt himself drop back. He opened his mouth quite widely.

"Wow, would you look at those pearly whites!" Pamela exclaimed. "You certainly take good care of your teeth, Mr. Wolfe!"

"Hnk hu!" Harry gurgled.

Dr. Stoker took a few moments to check his teeth. "Yes, you certainly have a bad break there, Mr. Wolfe. I'm afraid we won't be able to save the tooth. We'll have to pull it, but since you've got a healthy set of gums, I can replace it with a fake fang right away."

Harry gulped. "Will it hurt?"

"Oh no, I'll be giving you a dose of Novocain. You won't feel a thing!"

Harry smiled. "Oooohhh, Novocain!"

Dr. Stoker injected the Novocain into Harry's gums and allowed the numbing to take place. He and Pamela then went to work removing the fang and replacing it with a new one.

Half an hour later, Harry was looking at his new fang in the mirror. "Hey cool, a steel fang!"

Dr. Stoker smiled. "Yep, you'll be the talk of the town, that's for sure."

"Thank you so much, Doctor! I won't be breaking that tooth on a dumb old cat, that's for sure!"

Dr. Stoker laughed. "Oh don't worry, you won't!"

Harry and Elvira settled the payment with the receptionist and left.

"I feel great!" Harry said. "I think this is going to be one terrific Halloween!"

Elvira smiled. She linked her arm into Harry's and together they walked down the street.

Back at the dentist's office, Dr. Stoker and Pamela stood at the window and watched them walk away.

Pamela turned to Dr. Stoker. "Do you think it will work?"

"Of course! He thinks he's sporting a stainless steel fang." Dr. Stoker chuckled. "My great-great-great-great, er, how many greats was that?" He waved it away. "Doesn't matter, Grandfather Bram would be so proud of me.

Imagine the story he could write... his great-great-great-grandson replacing a werewolf's fang with a silver bullet!"

Pamela smiled. "When do you think he'll swallow it?"

"Next time he bites into a cat, I imagine." Dr. Stoker took a deep breath and let it out. "Well, I feel better already. That'll teach him to eat my cat!"

Mrs. C and the Sleigh

The sound of the crash awakens Snowball from her deep sleep. She groggily gets up and saunters outside her icy cave to investigate. She shakes her head, hoping that this is a dream, but unfortunately, it is all too real. There in front of her is Santa's sleigh, in a heap up against the cave's wall. Also in a heap are eight groaning reindeer, and one groaning Mrs. Claus.

The polar bear works her way over to the pile of creatures and begins to pull at the reins with her teeth, hoping to untangle her friends and get them on their feet again. After a few minutes of tugging, she manages to unravel some of the mess. Soon, the reindeer and Mrs. C are on their feet, shaken but unhurt.

Snowball slowly makes her way back to her cave, chuckling at yet another crazy antic here at Santa's Workshop. She'll have to ask the reindeer what happened. But for now, she has several weeks of sleep ahead of her.

Mrs. C looks at the lopsided and dented sleigh. She shakes her head. My, my, this doesn't look good, she thinks to herself. The reindeer all line up next to her, assessing the damage. My, my, this doesn't look good, they all think to themselves. Mrs. C walks up to the wall and begins to run her hands across it.

"I can never seem to find that dimensional opening," she mumbles as she continues her groping. "However does Mr. C do it?"

The reindeer gather up the reins of the sleigh and drag it towards the wall. They then walk into it, and through it, into another dimension where Santa's Workshop is secretly hidden from the rest of the world. Mrs. C stops her groping (she was a good ten feet off base anyway) and follows the decrepit sleigh into the wall.

They are greeted by a few elves who would normally park the sleigh in the garage and settle the reindeer in the stables. But today they come to a complete halt, shocked by the sight in front of them. Orion, one of the foremen, is the first to speak.

"Holy smokes, Mrs. C, what happened?"

"Well, I kind of missed the dimensional opening," she sputters. She looks around. "Um, where's Mr. C?"

"Fortunately for you, he's busy programming some computer games." Orion looks at the sleigh again. "Man, you're gonna get it!"

"I beg your pardon?" Mrs. C huffs. "I'm gonna get what?"

Orion blushes. "What I mean is, well, the sleigh is Mr. C's baby, you know."

"Orion, this is the new millennium. Women don't get heck from their husbands any more!" Mrs. C pauses uncertainly for a moment. "Do they?"

She sighs. "What am I going to do? This is Christmas Eve. And Mr. C doesn't even know that I took his sleigh."

"What?" Orion gasps. "You took it without his knowing?"

"Well, I knew he wouldn't like it!" She rolls her eyes. "He has this thing about women drivers for some reason."

"Gee, I wonder why," Orion says sarcastically.

"Ho, ho, ho!" Santa enters the garage, only to stop in his tracks when he sees the sleigh. "No, no, no!"

He turns to Mrs. C. "What happened here?"

"Ah, I had a little mishap." She burst into tears. "I'm so sorry. I should have told you I wanted to take it for a ride!"

A worried look crosses Santa's face. He grabs a hold of Mrs. C's arms. "Are you okay? Did you get hurt?"

"No," she sobs. "And the reindeer are fine. Just a little shook up is all."

Santa lets out a sigh of relief. "Well, thank goodness for that. Now, as for you, young lady..."

Mrs. C giggles through her tears. "Young lady, indeed."

Orion interrupts. "Ah, Mr. C, why don't you and Mrs. C go on into the workshop and have some tea and cookies. I'll get some of the guys to help me with the sleigh. We'll have it fixed up in no time." The other elves nodded in agreement.

"Good idea, Orion," Santa takes Mrs. C by the elbow and gently guides her towards the workshop. "The Mrs. and I are going to have a little chat."

Mrs. C looks back at Orion and winks. "Don't worry about me, Orion. I know how to sweet-talk this big lug."

The last thing Orion hears before the door closes behind them is Santa's loud "Harrumph!" He lets out a belly laugh as loud as the jolly fellow himself as he and the elves begin their repairs.

A while later, Santa and Mrs. C are sitting comfortably on the couch in Santa's workshop office sipping their tea. After a few minutes of silence, Mrs. C approaches the looming subject of the sleigh.

"I'm so sorry," she begins.

"You already said that," Santa interrupts her. "Don't worry about it." He chuckles. "Heck, I oversee the making of toys for millions of children all over the world. I'm sure I can take care of a damaged sleigh."

"But this is Christmas Eve! You've got to drive the sleigh tonight!"

Santa laughs. "Oh, I won't be driving the sleigh." He looks at Mrs. C. "You will!"

Mrs. C gasps. "What?"

"Well, you want to drive it so badly, you're going to so tonight. Heck woman, this is the new millennium! It's about time women started pulling their weight." He looks at Mrs. C again. "Aw, honeybunch, look at the stuff I've got to deliver. Gone are the days of rag dolls and wooden soldiers. Everyone wants computers and cell phones. Those technological gifts can get really heavy. I could use the help."

He gets down on one knee. "I've done this once before to ask you to be my wife and partner. Now I'm asking you once again to be my wife and partner."

Mrs. C smiles. "Of course I will!"

Later on that night, Santa and Mrs. C go back to the workshop garage and to find the sleigh and all the reindeer in excellent condition. The elves have already loaded up the toys and are waiting in a line to see Santa off. Santa helps Mrs. C into the sleigh and gets in after her. He picks up the reins and hands them to her.

"Are you sure about this?" she asks him.

"Yes I am." He decides not to tell her that he will be using a little Christmas magic to guide her along.

Mrs. C gives the reins a shake and the sleigh slides out of the garage. As it lifts off the ground, she feels it wobble, but then it straightens out into a smooth glide.

She turns to Santa. "Hey, I'm not so bad at this, am I?"

"No, you're not, my dear," he says as he releases a little magic dust. "No, you're not."

Snow Queen

"Here you go Mrs. C, one for you and one for me!" Chloe balanced the cups of hot chocolate, one in each hand, as she pushed the door open with her hip. She stopped short at the sight of Mrs. Claus's tears.

"Mrs. C, whatever is wrong?" In all the years the elf and Mrs. Claus have been the best of friends, Chloe had never seen her cry. She was always as jolly as Santa himself. Now she was sitting on her bed, crying and clutching what looked like a coat of animal skin. Chloe set the cups down and went to her.

"What happened? Did somebody hurt this animal?" She sat on the bed next to Mrs. C and put an arm around her shoulders.

"What?" Mrs. C sniffed. "Oh, you mean this." She held up the animal skin. "This is a sealskin. My sealskin"

Chloe gasped. "Then you really are a selkie!"

Mrs. C looked at Chloe. "You knew?"

Chloe blushed. "Well, there have always been rumours amongst the elves. You can go outside in the Arctic subzero temperatures with just your smock on and stay out there for hours. Even elfin magic limits our time outside. That's why we can never go with Santa on Christmas Eve." Chloe shrugged. "We figured if you were a selkie, you might've given Santa the ability to endure the cold like that."

Mrs. C shook her head. "No, Santa always had his own powers. But he did need the perfect match when he decided to marry. And that's where I came in."

She picked up her cup and took a sip. She sighed. "Mmm, you make the best hot chocolate, Chloe."

Chloe absently sipped at her own cup and stared at the sealskin now resting on Mrs. C's lap. She reached over and stroked the glossy fur. "So this is really yours?"

Mrs. C nodded. "Yes, it is. You see, a few centuries ago, Santa was a toy maker in a small town and he loved to make the local children happy by giving them toys on Christmas Eve. When the angels in Heaven realized what a good man he was, they approached him with the idea of making all the children in the world happy. He loved the idea, and so they flew him to the top of the Earth, where he could look down on his beloved children throughout the year. They brought him the elves and the reindeer, and then blessed the Workshop with extended life. In other words, everybody here would age, but very slowly."

She sipped her hot chocolate and continued. "Santa loved it here, but he was rather lonely. All the elves found mates amongst themselves, and happy as he was to marry them off, he envied them.

"Then one day, while he was exploring along the icy shores of the open Arctic Sea, he saw me. As you probably know, we selkies are seals who can come onto land and shed our skins to become human. We like to use our human forms to dance on the rocks. Or in my case, icebergs. You see, I'm from a large club of Arctic selkies." She sighed. "My name was, is, Snow Queen."

Chloe blinked. "Well, that explains why you never really had a name. We all call you Mrs. C, just as Santa does. Plus we never really knew where you came from. It's beginning to make sense now."

Mrs. C smiled. "Anyway, Santa saw me dancing on an iceberg and he knew right away that I was the woman for him. He also knew that, in order to take a selkie as a wife, a man must steal her sealskin. Since a selkie can't return to the water without it, she must follow the man home to become his wife."

"That's so barbaric!" Chloe exclaimed. "Oh, I mean..." she blushed and covered her mouth.

Mrs. C laughed. "Chloe, don't forget this happened centuries ago. These days, selkies are offered the option to stay with a man if she wishes to or not. But not back then. So, Santa stole my sealskin, and when my club went back into the water, I was left behind. So I followed Santa back to his workshop.

"He was a handsome man, and so sweet and kind. It didn't take me long to fall in love with him. Oh, I missed the sea life, but I was happy here too. When we married, Santa gave me my sealskin back and told me that if ever I was unhappy here, I could go back home and he'd understand.

"I put the sealskin away and never looked back." She sighed. "Until now. Just out of the blue, I got the urge to go back into the water. So I took the skin out. Just to see..." She burst into tears. "I don't know what to do."

Chloe put her arms around her friend. "There now, Mrs. C... Look, why don't you take your skin down to the sea and see how you feel about it then."

"But, what if I want to go back to the sea?"

"Then you go back. Santa said he'd understand."

Mrs. C got up. "You're right. I need to know for sure. I'm going to do it right now."

Chloe gulped. "Right now? Maybe you should sleep on it. Think about it for a few days."

"I need to do this now." Mrs. C hugged Chloe. "Thank you for being a good friend all these years. Perhaps I'll see you tomorrow. And perhaps I won't." She picked up her sealskin and left the room.

Chloe stood frozen for a moment, and then quickly left the cottage to find Santa.

"Santa! Santa!" Santa recognized Chloe's voice outside the workshop and went to the door. It narrowly missed hitting him as Chloe flew through it. "Santa! We have a big problem." She proceeded to tell him about the conversation she had with Mrs. C.

When she finished, Santa looked down and shook his head. "I wondered whether this day would ever come."

"Santa, you have to stop her! We can't lose her!"

"Chloe, it's her decision alone. All we can do is hope she makes the right one for both her and for us." He took his coat from the rack. "But I will follow her down to the sea. I need to know either way." He put a hand on Chloe's shoulder. "Thank you, Chloe. I'll be back." He left the workshop.

Several hours later, he was sitting behind a large chunk of ice, watching the sea. He could see Mrs. C standing at the edge of the water, sealskin in hand. She was singing an odd song, and he recalled hearing the same song when he first saw her as a selkie singing and dancing on the iceberg. He knew she was now Snow Queen, calling out to her club.

Suddenly, several seals jumped out of the water and onto the icy shore. They all unzipped their skins stepped out of them. He felt a moment of sadness as he realized that they had not aged as Mrs. C did.

The selkies seemed to have noticed the same thing. "Snow Queen!" One of them said. "What has happened to you?"

Snow Queen told them the story of the handsome young man who stole her sealskin, and with whom she fell in love with and stayed with happily all these centuries. "But as you can see, I have aged, albeit very slowly. I have lost my ability to stay young once I decided to stay on land."

The selkies all looked at each other. One of them stepped up to Snow Queen and placed a hand on her shoulder. "You are welcome to join us again, but you may not be happy amongst selkies so young."

Snow Queen nodded. "I'm concerned that I may not be able to keep up. But there is only one way to find out." Snow Queen opened her sealskin and stepped into it, as did the other selkies. Now in the form of seals, they all slipped into the water.

From behind the icy rock, Santa dropped his head into his hands. He sat there for a few hours, mourning the loss of his Snow Queen. He stood up, ready to head back to the workshop, when he heard a splash. He looked over to see a seal sitting on the shore. It lay down on the ice for a few moments to rest. Then it reached behind its back and unzipped its skin. Out of the skin stepped Snow Queen. She threw the sealskin aside and began to dance on the icy shore.

Santa understood. He snuck around the icy rocks to where the sealskin lay, and picked it up. With sealskin in hand, he headed back towards the workshop.

Chloe was pacing in front of the workshop door. When she saw Santa, her shoulders drooped. "She's gone, then," she said to Santa as he approached her.

"Not really." He held up the sealskin. "When a man steals a selkie's sealskin, she follows the man home to become his wife."

Just then, Snow Queen, who was now Mrs. C once again, approached the workshop. "I'm going home," she announced nonchalantly. "I've had an exhausting night." Chloe caught the twinkle in her eyes and smiled.

Santa yawned. "I think I'll call it a night as well. It's been a long one for me too." He took Mrs. C by the hand and the two of them made their way towards the cottage.

Chloe didn't fail to notice Santa passing the sealskin back to Mrs. C.

The Christmas Strike

Rudolf sat in his stall and looked out the window. "This is going to be a mess," he mumbled to himself as he watched the eight reindeer walk in an endless circle around Santa's sleigh. Around the reindeer was a bigger circle made up of dozens of elves. Santa stood outside the circles, along with the two elf foremen. They were talking to the circling elves and reindeer. Rudolf couldn't hear what they were saying, but he could only imagine.

He knew that the reindeer were on strike. As members of the F.R.F. (Flying Reindeer Federation) they'd presented Santa with some demands. He wasn't sure what those demands were, but it seemed Santa refused to honour them, so the reindeer walked off the job early this morning. And the elves, being members of the E.L.F. (Elfin Labour Federation), walked with them in show of support.

"I'm so glad I'm part-time," he said to himself. He wasn't a union member, but he was fortunate enough to reap the benefits of the other reindeer. He often wondered why the elves and reindeer even had unions since nobody at the North Pole had, or needed money. With magic, Santa had always been able to supply the best comfort they could possibly have. And now they were on strike. Whatever for?

He could see Santa throw up his arms and walk away. The non-union foremen followed him. The trio seemed to be headed towards the reindeer stall. Rudolf realized they were coming to see him. He would finally have an answer to what was going on, but he couldn't help the sense of foreboding he was getting. What did Santa want from him, he wondered. He went to the stall door to greet them.

"Rudolph, we need your help," Santa said. "We need to set up talks with the reindeer and elves, and I could use some extra non-union members at the table."

Rudolph shook his head. "Wouldn't it be a conflict of interest? I am a reindeer."

"We need your opinion as a non-union member," Charlie, one of the foremen, said.

"And we need it fast," chimed in Billie, the other foreman. "This is Christmas Eve and we haven't even loaded up the sleigh yet!"

"I don't even know what they're striking for," Rudolf said.

Santa snorted. "You won't believe this. They want organic hay."

Rudolph blinked. "Organic hay?"

"And spring water!" Charlie added.

"I don't get it," Rudolph said. "The elves grow our hay in the hothouses, and our water comes from the snow and ice here."

"Polluted snow and ice," Billie added. "We're living on the Arctic Ocean, remember? Between that and all the polluted air we get from North America and Asia, we have a problem. And since we water the timothy grass with the same stuff we drink, well, the hay is full of nasty chemicals."

"Oh." Rudolph turned to Santa. "But we're immortal. It's not going to kill us."

"Ah, but it can make us weak and ill." Santa sighed. "And I can't even use my magic to make it clean. It's beyond repair. All we can do is reverse the damage. And that'll take decades!" He sighed again. "We've never had a strike before. I just don't know what to do."

Rudolph nodded. "Okay, let's go talk to them. Maybe we can work something out."

They went back to the picket line. The elves and reindeer saw them approach and stopped marching. They held their circles.

Donner, the union president, stepped forward. He looked at Rudolph, and then looked at Santa "I hope you're not planning to bring in scabs."

"Huh?" Santa looked puzzled. "Oh, you mean Rudolph. Well, I do have deliveries to make tonight. If I have to, I'll get Elizabeth and her gang in to help."

Donner laughed. "Liz and her girls? Come on, Santa, they're cows, not reindeer. Yeah, they're cute in that milk commercial they made with you, but they can't deliver presents. It'll never fly. Pardon the pun."

"Then I'll use Rudolph to guide them."

Rudolph gasped. "What? Wait a minute, I'm not crossing that picket line!"

Donner smiled. "Smart kid." He turned to Santa. "So have you thought about our demands?"

Santa shook his head. "Donner, I can't afford to bring in organic hay. Even if we were able to grow our own, I'd have to get special organic soil, not to mention boatloads of spring water. My magic is limited. I need it to keep the elves stocked with materials for toy-making."

Charlie stepped up. "As it is, Santa had to go all out these last few years. Kids want computer games and all these other e-toys. He's had to retrain the elves as electronic geeks."

"And if Santa starts throwing his magic around, we won't have enough for toy-making, not to mention getting you guys up and flying!" Billie added.

Santa shrugged. "Look, I'm just as worried about the environment as you are. Heck, I even quit smoking my corncob pipe years ago in order to keep our air clean, not to mention to set an example for the children. And I've had that pipe for centuries! It wasn't easy..."

"Cookies and hot chocolate for everyone!"

Santa turned towards his workshop to see Mrs. Claus pushing a large cart overflowing with thermoses, cups and cookies.

"What are you doing, dear?" He called to her.

"Just helping out the strikers." She stopped the cart by the picket line. "The poor dears are probably freezing out here."

Santa rolled his eyes. "My own wife fraternizing with the enemy." He watched as the circles broke up and everyone gathered at the cart. He then looked over at the now freed-up sleigh.

"Don't even think about it!" Donner said.

Santa raised his eyebrows. "You know I could just weave a little magic and lift that sleigh right out of your picket line."

Donner smiled. "Ah, but you won't. You're a fair man. And that's why I know you will come up with an acceptable solution to our demands."

Santa shook his head. He turned and headed towards the workshop. Charlie and Billie followed. Rudolph looked back at Donner. "Don't worry, we'll figure something out." He followed the trio back to the workshop.

Once inside, they sat around the empty table. All the toys were finished and stacked up in the warehouse, ready to be loaded onto the sleigh. It didn't matter that the sleigh was being picketed; he needed the elves to load it. And even if they weren't picketing, he would still need the reindeer to fly it.

He looked at the clock. Only a few more hours left until midnight. He was able to suspend time while he delivered all the toys. With millions of children's homes to visit, he needed all the extra time. But he couldn't keep midnight from coming. He sighed.

An hour later, Donner joined them. "Any solutions?"

They had all spent the hour watching the clock. Nobody had said a word. Nobody had any ideas.

Rudolph turned to Donner. Can't you put off this strike until after Christmas? You know how disappointed the children will be if Santa doesn't deliver."

"Sorry kid, but that's how strikes work. You walk just before the company's most crucial time."

"This isn't some dang company, Donner! It's Christmas!" Rudolph took a deep breath and let it out slowly. He was determined not to lose his temper.

Donner looked sad. "I know, kid. It isn't fair. If it were up to me, I'd postpone the talks and get everybody back to work. But the union members voted to strike." He sat down at the table and for the next couple of hours, said nothing as well.

The clock struck 11:00. Rudolph got up and walked around the workshop. He noticed Santa's corncob pipe sitting on the shelf, collecting dust. He briefly smiled at the fond memory of poor Santa going through withdrawals when he quit smoking it. He'd even tried to put a filter on the pipe to stop the harsh chemicals from coming through, in hopes that it would frustrate him enough to quit easily. Rudolph picked the pipe up and looked at the crudely made filter.

Filter. Of course! Why didn't anybody think of this!

He turned back to the table. "I have the solution!"

Ten minutes later the group emerged from the workshop and approached the picket line. Donner stepped up to the picketers and announced, "We have a solution. Rudolph will explain, and then we can vote on it."

Rudolph cleared his throat. "Importing spring water can be very costly to Santa's magic. So I figured, why not simply clean our own water?" He looked at the elves. "You've been trained in electronics. All you have to do is design and build a complex water filter system that will remove all harmful chemicals."

"We have the smarts to do it," Billie added. "And it would take a minimal amount of magic."

"And once the water is clean, the hay will be organic," Santa said. "And if we do this, I can afford the right soil."

The elves and reindeer gathered together for a few moments to discuss the proposal. Then they all turned to Donner, who said, "All in favour, say aye."

"Aye!" It was a unanimous vote.

"Okay then, the strike is officially over," Donner said. "Let's do Christmas!"

Everybody cheered. With barely a few minutes to go, they all ran to the warehouse to begin loading the sleigh.

By midnight, the toys were all loaded, the reindeer were strapped in and Santa was sitting in his sleigh. He turned to Rudolph. "It's a clear night, but you're welcome to come with us anyway."

Rudolph shook his head. "Not this time, Santa. It's been a long day and I haven't even had any of Mrs. Claus's cookies yet."

Santa ho-ho-hoed. "The night has just begun, Rudolph! But thank you for saving Christmas."

Rudolph smiled. "Oh, it wasn't me, Santa. It was your corncob pipe and the memories it brought."

"Well, I knew there must've been a reason I kept it after all these years," Santa said. "Who'd have thought it would be to give us clean water."

With another ho-ho-ho, he shook the reins and the sleigh lifted off the ground. Like a streak of lightning, it disappeared into the starlit sky.

Rudolph looked at the pipe he was still holding and smiled. He then headed back to the workshop to put it back on the shelf. And to get his fill of Mrs. Claus's cookies.

*Mermaids and Lions
and
Other Mortal Creatures*

At the Pound

It's a warm, sunny day here at the Pound; a nice break from the weeks of cold, rainy weather autumn tends to bring us. Today, we're allowed to stay out a little longer to welcome the warmth of the sunshine on our arthritic bones. Maisy, Tinkerbell and I have been here in the slammer for countless months. At least we think it's been months; we're dogs what do we know?

My name is Golda, a pretty name until you realize that I'm a Golden Retriever. Then the eye-rolling starts. I get it from every dog that comes through this place. My ex-masters thought it was cute. They even thought I was cute. Until their son started sneezing every time he hugged me. Then they had to get rid of me. I won't even go into the heart-wrenching separation. It left me listless and depressed for weeks. I sat in the corner of my cage and wouldn't even get up to check out any of the potential masters who came by looking for a dog to adopt. Just as well. I couldn't stand another heartbreak. Even if it means that I will eventually be put on death row. It's inevitable; I'm getting old.

As is Maisy. She got thrown in the slammer about the same time I did. She's a big, black, burly Lab and something-or-other mix. She was adopted by a sweet, little old lady who keeled over just days after she brought Maisy home. Poor Maisy; she was locked in the house with that dead woman for three days until another neighbour complained about her continuous barking. She was pretty dehydrated by the time she got here. Since then, she's been in and out of here several times. The humans like her at first, but her playfulness causes a lot of torn furniture and broken vases. Once she accidentally knocked a little girl down the stairs when she jumped on her to lick her face. Not a good track record. She's no longer up for adoption, which means she'll be on death row soon. Fortunately, the humans here like her so they keep pushing the date back.

And then there's Tinkerbell. Some Pound officer thought it would be cute to name the poor Chihuahua after Paris Hilton's dog. She was a runaway. No one knows who she is, or where she came from. She refuses to talk about it. We don't understand the humans too well when they talk about us, but from what we gathered, Tink was abused on a regular basis. She came in looking scrawny and broken. Maisy and I befriended her, and being much bigger dogs, we tend to be protective of her. Which means that we growl whenever humans come near her. Then we laugh at the baffled look on their faces. Tink is understandably afraid of humans. She's much younger than us and may some day be without our protection.

And that's what we are discussing on this fine afternoon in the Pound's outdoor yard. Tinkerbell is running a few laps around the yard, while Maisy and I sit off to one side, soaking in the sun.

"I used to have energy like that," Maisy reminisces. "All those floors I slid across…"

"And all the walls you slammed into!" I retort. "Even now, you're still knocking down the Pound officers."

"Well, it's not my fault they don't brace themselves for my onslaught!" She pauses for a moment. "Golda, what is Tink going to do once we're gone?"

"I don't know," I answer. "She won't go near a human. Poor thing shivers even when the pound folks come around. And they don't come any kinder than that!" I watch as Tink speeds by us. "Hah, we could always try to find her a man!"

"Are you kidding? She hears a man's voice, she cowers in terror!"

"Not a human man, Maisy, a dog man!"

"A dog man? Ooohhh," Maisy ponders for a moment, and then looks at me. "Uh, kinda hard to find one that, you know, can do it. If they're not neutered when they come in here, they will be."

"I don't mean for that, you bonehead! Companionship, that's what I'm talking about." I shake my head. "Gees, Maisy, your mind is always in the gutter."

"Best place to find fire hydrants," Maisy muses. She looks over at the two terriers nestled together in the corner of the yard. "You know, I hear old Scotty over there is up for death row any time now. I hear he is having major health problems." She shakes her head.

"Such a shame. Mrs. S will be so devastated. I bet she'll die of a broken heart."

"You can always tell when one of us is going to be put down. The Pound officers have such a forlorn look on their faces." I look back towards the building. "Are they done doing the cats yet?"

"I think so. Gee, I almost feel sorry for those ornery critters."

"Now now, Maisy, critters is critters!" I make a face. "Huh, even cats!"

Tinkerbell comes over to us. "Whoo!" she huffs. "What a workout!" She looks around. "Say, I heard Sammy and

Jonesy talking. They said there's a couple of new dogs coming in today." She giggles. "I hope one of them's a cute fella!"

"Tink!" Maisy is surprised. "I didn't know you were interested in meeting guys! Ah, you know the ones in here, they can't, um, do it..."

"Sheesh, Maisy, get your head out of the gutter! I'm just looking for companionship!"

She chuckles. "Besides, sometimes instinct takes over. Heh heh, we don't know what we're doing, but it feels good anyway."

"Who's head is in the gutter now?" Maisy huffs. She looks towards the gate, which the officers are opening. "Ah, here come our new inmates now."

Two Chihuahuas slowly enter the yard. All the dogs stop what they are doing and look over. Sammy and Jonesy each put on their tough Doberman look and saunter towards them. Tinkerbell joins them.

"Now don't go being bullies, guys!" she tells them.

"Now, what do you take us for?" Sammy says. "I'm insulted! Besides, they're as small as you are. We don't pick on wimps!"

"Wimps! Why you..." but the Dobermans walk away from her and towards the Chihuahuas. Tink catches up to them.

"Welcome to the slammer," Sammy says to them. The dogs all do the mandatory butt sniffing. Sammy continues, "What are you in for?"

"A noise complaint. Me and my sister here tend to get a little loud when we chat. And since our master worked night shift, well, that's when we yakked. The neighbours didn't like it. Oh, but don't worry," the new dog hurries to say, "We won't keep youse guys up or nothing!" He introduces himself. "My name is Taco. Ah, my sister is Belle." He rolls his eyes. "Isn't that sick. I can never understand human humour!"

Sammy and Jonesy look at each other, then burst out laughing. I can't help but feel a sense of relief that someone else has a funnier name than mine. I look over at Tink and see that she is staring at Taco. Taco is staring back at her.

Maisy is chuckling. "Heh, heh, Tinkerbell, Taco, Belle... the names that breed gets."

I nudge her and point towards the dogs. "Ah, Maisy, look at Tink. I think she's in love."

Tink and Taco are nose to nose, tails wagging furiously. Belle leaves her brother and his new lady, and joins Sammy and Jonesy for a chat.

I look back at Maisy. "Well, still worried about her?"

Maisy laughs. "Not a chance. I think she can hold her own. Besides, Sammy and Jonesy act tough, but they'll look out for her." She looks towards the building and nudges me. I look over and see a Pound officer come out.

"Oh no," I feel a tightening in my stomach. "He's got that look."

The officer goes over to the terriers, gently picks up Scotty and carries him into the building. Mrs. S lets out a heart-wrenching howl.

"Noooo, not my Scotty!" she yells, and then collapses. Maisy and I run over to her. We both lay down on each side of her and nuzzle her.

"There, there, Mrs. S, easy now." Maisy continues to console her as Sammy waves me over.

He whispers quietly to me. "I hear they are doing a few dogs today." He sighs and shakes his head. "What is this world coming to?"

I can't help but get an ominous feeling in the pit of my stomach. The door opens once again, and two more officers come out. One goes over to Mrs. S and picks her up.

"It's just as well," Sammy says quietly. "The poor dear!" Then he looks over my shoulder in terror. "No!" he gasps.

Just as I turn around to look, I feel myself being lifted by a pair of strong arms. Sammy growls, and Jonesy and Maisy both run over to join him, ready to pounce on the officer.

"No!" I yell. "They'll do all three of you for that! Tinkerbell needs you!" The officer slowly carries me towards the building. "Please take good care of her!"

The last thing I hear is their promise that Tinkerbell would be fine. And maybe it's my imagination, but I think I hear the little Chihuahua's voice saying, "I love you, Golda!"

The Mission

Sir Wynston balanced himself on one knee, head bowed. "Please, your Highness, you must get down off of Korny. I have a mission to get to."

"No!" Princess Verda remained seated on the unicorn, gingerly swinging Wynston's sword through the air. She brought the sword down and pulled a rose out from her belt. She tossed it at Wynston and smiled.

"Princess, if I don't get my men together soon, your father will have my head!" Wynston shuddered at the thought. Although a fair ruler, King Lizzo did not take kindly to disobedient knights, especially when such an important task was at hand.

He tried to reason with the stubborn princess. "Look, the gimlins have to be destroyed. They have been eating our crops and scaring our livestock away. They multiply like those rabbits we read about in those Third Dimension fables. The longer we wait, the worse it will get."

"And I won't let you do it!" Verda shouted. She took a deep breath and spoke calmly. "The gimlins are adorable creatures. I can't let you slaughter them. There must be another way to control the situation."

Just as Wynston was about to speak, they were surrounded by several gimlins. Being avid tree climbers, they scurried up the unicorn with little effort. Wynston found one perched on his shoulder. Verda giggled as one cuddled within her ample bosom.

"This is ridiculous!" Wynston stood up and shooed away the gimlin on his shoulder. Korny began to whinny as another gimlin began humping his back leg. Wynston shooed that one away as well.

He looked at Verda and felt a twinge of jealousy as yet another gimlin cuddled by her breast. There had always been a certain attraction between him and the princess. She was of marriageable age, but, being a lowly knight, the king would not consider him a worthy husband for his beautiful daughter.

At this moment, however, all he felt was frustration. As he was preparing to go on the gimlin-destroying mission, she came by on the pretence of seeing him off. She then sat on the unicorn and told him that she would not get off until he found an alternate method of gimlin-control. Wynston sighed. She was quite the animal activist. He should have seen it coming.

He took Korny's reins and began walking the unicorn out of the courtyard. Verda dropped the gimlin she was playing with and looked at Wynston.

"What are you doing?" she asked him.

"The king told me to do something, and by gosh, I'm going to do it!" he retorted. He stopped walking for a moment and looked at Verda.

"Princess," he said, "you are going on a gimlin-destroying mission with me."

Verda gasped. "You can't be serious!"

Wynston began walking again. "Oh, I'm very serious."

He walked for several miles with Korny obediently at his side and Verda sitting pensively on him. They were headed towards the valley, where the gimlins liked to nest. Wynston was to meet his army of men, and together they were to slaughter the colony. He wasn't thrilled at the prospect. Verda was right; they were adorable creatures. But their appetite for the crops had to be taken into consideration. He had heard about the locusts in the Third

Dimension world. Apparently, they were much smaller than gimlins, but just as destructive. He was determined to keep the same thing from happening to this world.

Several hours later, they arrived at the edge of the escarpment overlooking the valley. They had accumulated gimlins along the way and had an entourage of at least one hundred, most of them scrambling to get close to the princess. And she was enjoying every minute of it. Wynston sighed and shook his head. He then caught sight of his men coming towards them. All six of them.

Verda stared at the small group. She then looked at Wynston. "That's it? That's your army?"

Wynston shrugged. "Our dimension has been at peace for several centuries now. We don't really need an army."

Verda began to laugh. "How do you expect to slaughter thousands of gimlins with an army of seven? I can't understand my father even suggesting such a thing!"

Wynston was thoughtful for a moment. He grinned sheepishly. "Come to think of it, the king didn't quite use the word 'slaughter.' He just told me to get rid of these pests."

"Huh, just as I thought," Verda said. "To think you were actually contemplating killing these poor creatures. Well, I guess we'd better come up with a plan."

Verda, Wynston and the six soldiers stood at the edge of the escarpment and looked out over the valley. The plush green ground was heavily populated with gimlins. The plants grew as quickly as the gimlins ate them, but the animals were quickly overpopulating the plants, and they were moving out into the farmlands.

"Hmm, I wonder," Verda said. "Do you think we could get them to go back to the valleys where they originally came from?"

Wynston stared at her. "And how do you propose we do that? We don't exactly have a pied piper like those humans do."

Verda giggled as the gimlins climbed up Korny and onto her to settle on her lap. The weight was too much for the poor unicorn and he fell sideways, dumping the princess and the gimlins onto the ground.

Wynston helped her up. He chuckled. "Perhaps we could use you as bait and get these animals to follow you back to their valleys."

Verda stared at him and blinked. "Wynston, what a wonderful idea!"

"Oh, uh, Princess, I was just joking!" Wynston stuttered. "Your father would never go for that."

"Nonsense! He wants to be rid of these creatures and the only way to do it is to remove them and place them elsewhere." Verda climbed back on Korny. "Now, let's head towards the gimlins' valleys. It will take a few days, but I know we can do it!"

The soldiers all looked at one another and then at Verda. One of them said, "Well, I don't know about the gimlins, but I'll be more than happy to follow milady anywhere!"

The others agreed and soon they were off, leading the parade of gimlins towards their new, albeit original home. As they travelled along, more and more gimlins caught sight of the princess and joined the procession. Soon the valley was empty. They spent the next three days travelling and setting up camp in the evenings. Fortunately for the soldiers, gimlins were heavy sleepers and everyone woke up refreshed and ready to move on.

On the fourth day, they arrived at the gimlins' valleys. The gimlins were so excited to see the abundance of greenery, they quickly headed down into the valleys without a second thought to their beloved Princess Verda. Wynston and the soldiers each breathed a sigh of relief as they began their quiet journey back home with the subdued princess on Korny's back.

King Lizzo was impressed with the mission and decided to offer Wynston his daughter's hand in marriage.

The happy princess retired to her room to rest after the long journey. She lay down on her bed and reached down into her large bosom. She pulled out the gimlin she had hidden there before she left the valley. She knew she shouldn't have kept it, but she wanted one for a pet. And after all, one gimlin was harmless, wasn't it?

What the princess didn't know was that she chose a pregnant female who would be giving birth to five gimlins on the eve of her wedding day.

Blue Haze

The morning was bright. Topaz blinked as she entered the outside world, her younger sister Daisy in tow. They stopped at the doorway for a moment to take in the colourful world around them, but were quickly pushed aside.

"Out of the way ladies, there's work to be done!" Several women jostled them as they left the hive. "You won't be able to collect pollen from those flowers by just staring at them."

Topaz and Daisy quickly took flight and joined the women as they made their way to work the fields. Soon the air was buzzing with activity as the bees went from flower to flower.

"Why do we have to do all the work?" Daisy asked her sister as they sat on a buttercup. Topaz sighed. She had been training her young sibling for several days now, but it has become a tedious job as Daisy continually fired a barrage of questions at her.

"Because we're women, Daisy. The women are the workers. The drones just sit around and wait for the Queen to pick her mate," she explained, and then muttered, "the useless pests..."

"What do you mean, useless? I entertain you, don't I?" Topaz and Daisy turned to see a drone resting lazily on a flower near by. He got up and flew over to the two girls. "Here, need some help?" He picked up a bead of pollen and tossed it to Topaz.

"Get a life, will you, Drake?" Topaz stuffed the pollen in her pouch. "I'm so glad I'm not a queen. I'd never be able to put up with the likes of you."

Drake chuckled and quickly snatched the girls' pouches from them as he flew away. With shouts of anger, Topaz and Daisy chased the playful drone. He stopped suddenly, causing both girls to crash into him. The three bees somersaulted mid-air.

"Hey, what is that?" Drake was staring out at the horizon. "Looks like some sort of haze."

Topaz grabbed the two pouches from him. "The only haze I see here is around that empty head of yours!"

"No, Topaz, he's right!" Daisy pointed towards the horizon. "There is a haze out there. It looks kind of blue."

The bees stared at the haze for a few moments. "What is that?" Topaz echoed Drake's question.

"There's only one way to find out," Drake said and started flying towards the haze. "You ladies coming?"

"Drake, no, it's too far away," Daisy called after him. "We're not supposed to wander far from the hive!" She looked over at Topaz.

Topaz sighed. "Come on, let's see if we can keep him out of trouble." They quickly followed the curious drone.

They travelled for several hours, stopping occasionally to rest on a flower and drink from its dew. Topaz's worry changed to curiosity as they flew closer to the blue haze. The sun rose higher as the morning passed, changing the blue to a dull brown. Soon they were able to detect some wave-like movements in the haze.

The three bees stopped to study the mysterious cloud. "It looks like it's alive," Topaz commented. "We shouldn't get too close. Oh look, maybe we could ask these fellas if they know what it is."

A couple of odd-looking bugs were flying towards them from the direction of the cloud.

"Well, aren't you a colourful trio!" one of the bugs called out to them. "What's with the stripes?"

"We're bees," Drake told them. "What are you, some kind of grasshoppers?"

The two bugs looked at each other and chuckled. "I guess you can say that," one of them said. "We're locusts. We'd introduce ourselves, but we have no names. There's just too many of us, so we don't bother naming our kind."

The three bees looked out at the dark cloud. It seemed to be getting closer. They gasped as realization dawned on them at the same time. "That cloud is a bunch of bugs?" Daisy whispered.

The locusts laughed out loud. "A bunch of bugs. That's an understatement!"

Topaz noticed the barren fields below the locust cloud. "What's happening to all the plants?"

"Oh, we're eating them." The locusts noticed the shocked looks on the bees' faces. "Hey, I know it ain't pretty, but we're just trying to survive. Look, why don't you join us? It's an easy life. We just eat and play."

"Sounds like fun to me," Drake started flying towards the cloud. "Come on, girls, it beats collecting pollen all day!"

"Drake, no! They're destroying all the plants and flowers! Daisy!" Topaz's protests fell on deaf ears as Daisy followed Drake and the two locusts. She sighed and followed the group to the edge of the cloud.

The cloud had slowly turned into a flurry of bugs hunting for food. The ground was covered in a carpet of locusts, all busy in their feeding frenzy. Those in the air were moving to fresh feeding grounds where plants and flowers were still green and plentiful. The three bees landed on a wild rose bush.

"This looks like fun," Daisy said as she hunted for sweet nectar. "And we don't even have to worry about bringing pollen back to the hive."

"Hey, this is our flower!" Drake shouted at a group of locusts that landed on the bush and began to devour it.

"You snooze, you loose, buddy!" one of them shouted back. The group laughed and continued with their feast.

One of the two locusts that they originally met joined them on the flower. "You may want to hurry with your meal," he told the bees. "We locusts tend to be somewhat gluttonous, since we don't have a very long life."

"What do you mean?" Topaz was getting worried.

"Well, those big monsters will be here to spray stuff on us and kill us."

Topaz gasped. "What big monsters?"

"Why humans, of course."

"But I thought humans liked bugs! They're always collecting our honey. And we don't mind sharing with them; there's plenty for everyone." Topaz shook her head. "Why would they want to kill you?"

"I guess they don't like the way we take their crops." The locust rolled his eyes. "Obviously, they don't like to share their food with us!"

"Can't say I blame them. Look at what you're doing to all the plants and flowers!"

"Hey, like I said, we're just trying to survive!"

A humming sound cut through the din of the buzzing locusts. It was getting louder. The locust looked up and pointed. "See that flying thing? That's a human with killer spray coming this way." He looked at Topaz. "You may want to get out of here." The locust jumped on a flower and ravenously chewed at it, enjoying his last moments of life.

Topaz sprung into action. She located Drake on another flower and grabbed his arm. "We've got to get out of here!"

"Are you kidding? This is great!" Drake went back to his feasting.

"Listen, Drake, if we don't leave now, we're going to die!" She pointed to the flying machine coming towards them. "That thing will kill us!"

Drake felt a sense of dread in the pit of his stomach. "Okay, we're fast flyers, we can do this." He looked around. "Where's Daisy?"

They looked around, but couldn't spot the yellow and black bee in the cloud of brown bugs. They frantically began to call her name. "Daisy! *Daaaiiisy!*"

"What?" Daisy flew up to them.

Topaz breathed a sigh of relief. "We've got to get out of here before that flying machine kills us!"

Daisy stared at the oncoming machine for a moment. Then she started laughing. "Don't be silly, that's just a big bird." She continued to chew on a rose petal.

"Daisy, we have to go! Now!" Topaz and Drake tried to drag Daisy along with them as the flying machine came upon them.

"Okay, okay, lead the way!" Daisy got up to follow them out of the bustling cloud. They flew with speed and didn't stop until they were well clear of the killing machine.

Drake and Topaz landed on a nearby flower to catch their breath. They looked back for Daisy, but didn't see her. Topaz panicked. "Drake, where is she?"

"I don't know," Drake flew around to take a look. "I haven't seen her since we left the locusts. I assumed she was right behind us."

Topaz sat on the flower, head down and wings drooping. "Oh no, not my sister!"

Drake and Topaz sat on the flower for the rest of the day and watched as the blue haze slowly gave way to a clear sky and barren fields. They mourned the loss of their friend and sister. And they mourned the loss of the thousands of locusts who were just trying to survive.

The Sleeping Cave

"Good morning, Mary!" Uncle Sal, cheerful as usual, placed a cup of steaming coffee in front of me, even though the muggy July morning promised a hot summer day. I yawned and began to eat the oatmeal he lovingly prepared for me every morning for the last two years since Aunt Beatrice died.

"Uncle Sal, have I ever told you how good your oatmeal tastes?"

"Only every morning," he replied. We both laughed. This had become our morning greeting, one of our ways of dealing with our grief since my aunt's death. Aunt Bea and Uncle Sal were childless and took me in when my parents died from an influenza outbreak when I was a child. Every morning before going to school, I helped with the chores around the farm. They made sure I finished high school. After all, this was 1905 and an educated woman had a better chance of marrying well.

They were disappointed, but soon accepted the fact that I fell in love with Rory, a local farmer. They accepted our decision to get married, and I was extremely happy, until the tragedy struck. Rory accidentally stepped on a rusty nail. The infection in his foot caused him to lose his leg from the knee down. Much as I proclaimed my love regardless of the loss, Rory decided I should find a more worthy husband. Then he disappeared.

This would sound like a typically tragic love story, except that he wasn't the only person to disappear. There were at least a dozen people in the area, all of them afflicted with some sort of illness, who had disappeared. I wasn't sure whether he had met the same fate as they had.

"Mary, are you okay?" Uncle Sal looked concerned.

"Sorry, Uncle Sal, I was just daydreaming," I assured him.

"Well, better wake up then, we've got some work to do!"

The sun had started to come up, so I snuffed the oil lamp. "I hear that lots of cities are providing electricity in people's homes these days," I said, as I pulled on my boots.

"Be a while before we see it around here," Uncle Sal replied. "If we ever see it."

We headed toward barn. I opened the door and readied myself for Daisy's onslaught. She was my pet goat. I helped Uncle Sal birth her when I was younger. We had lost her mother in the process, so I nursed her with a baby bottle and weaned her as she got older. We became fast friends, and she now followed me around as I did my daily chores. She would always await me at the barn door every morning. Except this morning. There was no Daisy at the door. I looked around the barn. There was no sign of Daisy.

Uncle Sal noticed as well. "Where's Daisy? Did you put her in last night?"

"Yes, I did," I replied. I moved through the barn and looked in every corner, worried that I might find her ill or even dead. But I couldn't find her at all. I panicked. "Where is she?"

"She must've gotten out somehow," Uncle Sal said. "Now don't worry, Mary, she's never wandered far. We'll find her."

We spent the whole morning looking for her. We went to the neighbouring farms, asking if anyone saw her, then looking around some more. By noon, we were back at the farm, empty-handed.

Uncle Sal shook his head. "First, people begin disappearing. Now, animals... What next?"

I looked at him. "You don't think she's met with the same fate, do you?"

"Who knows? Folks around here are saying that Martians are kidnapping people. Maybe they're taking animals now too." He looked at me. "I think that science feller has something to do with all this."

"Who, Mr. Wilfred?" I thought about the eccentric man who was always coming up with strange inventions. The son of a farmer, he spent his days in the fields and his evenings reading science fiction books.

"Well, Albert Einstein is his hero," Uncle Sal chuckled. "Now there's a feller who can come up with all sorts of funny stuff. The theory of relativity, whatever that is. I always thought of you and me as relativities... We're related, right?"

I laughed. "Yes Uncle Sal, I'm proud to say we are. And I have a great idea. I'm going to go pay Mr. Wilfred a visit. He seems like a smart man; maybe he has some idea of what has happened to these people, and maybe to Daisy."

Uncle Sal looked worried. "Oh honey, are you sure that's a good idea? He's a bit odd."

"And that's why nobody has thought to seek his help," I said. "Don't worry, he's quite harmless. I'll just saddle up Ol' Punkins and ride over to his farm." I got up and kissed Uncle Sal on the cheek. "I'll be back soon."

An hour later, I was making my way up the lane to Mr. Wilfred's farm. I could see him in the far field with some animals. He seemed to be leading them towards the wooded area. He had a couple of cows with him, along with a goat that looked a lot like Daisy. I strained my memory, but couldn't recall him having goats on his farm. I felt a sense of dread. Maybe Uncle Sal was right about him. I decided to follow Mr. Wilfred into the woods.

I stayed far enough behind him so that he wouldn't see me. We moved at a slow pace, him because of the cows, me because of Ol' Punkins, my aging mare. Eventually, we came to an open, hilly area. Mr. Wilfred led the animals to the side of a steep hill. He stepped towards the side of the hill, put his hands into the side of the hill, and pulled open the side of the hill. I rubbed my eyes and stared at the illusion. He was shooing the animals into the opening. Without a second thought, I brought Ol' Punkins to a gallop and reached the opening just as it was beginning to close. I jumped off my horse and ran in, just as it closed.

Mr. Wilfred looked at me. "What are you doing here?"

"I should ask you the same thing," I answered. I was then knocked off balance, but soon regained my footing as the goat began to nuzzle me.

"Daisy!" I yelled. I stared at Mr. Wilfred. "What are you doing with my goat?"

Mr. Wilfred sighed. "You might as well come with me and I'll show you."

Holding a lamp, he led us through a long, dark passageway, and into a cave. He put the lamp down and lit several more around the cave. I could see a large, strange-looking opening in the side of the cave. It gave off an eerie glow.

"I was just about to leave," Mr. Wilfred led the cows to the opening; then he turned to me. "But now that you know my secret, you'll have to come with me."

"Come where?" I asked. I went towards the opening, throwing all caution to wind in favour of my curiosity. Daisy followed me.

Mr. Wilfred took me by the wrist. "You'll see." He pulled me into the opening, the ever-faithful Daisy following along. As I stepped into the dark opening, I felt myself fall asleep.

I wasn't sure how long I'd been asleep when I felt Daisy's head butting my back. I opened my eyes and looked around. I was lying outside the opening in the side of the hill, with Mr. Wilfred and the cows. They were awake.

"Good grief," I mumbled. "I feel like I've slept for a hundred years!"

Mr. Wilfred looked at me. "You have, my dear. Welcome to the future!"

"Huh?"

"We are now in the future. This is the year 2005."

Now I knew he was crazy. I took a hold of Daisy's collar and started to head back to the farm. Ol' Punkins was gone, and I assumed she had gone back already.

Mr. Wilfred took hold of the two cows and began to follow me. "Please let me explain," he called after me. Once again my curiosity took hold of me, and I turned back towards him.

"Time travel is impossible!" I yelled at him.

"We didn't really time travel. You see, that entrance led to a time warp. Everything in it was at a stand-still, while the rest of the world carried on. It was dark in there, so you couldn't see all the others that were there. We all fell asleep for a hundred years."

I stared at him. "Are you telling me that all those missing people were in that cave?"

"Yes. They were all ill, so I decided to have them sleep and wake up in a future where their illnesses might be cured." He smiled. "They've already gone out into the new world to find their cures. New medicines, artificial limbs, and you should see what they've done with electricity! I've done some exploring while you were still sleeping... it's a wonderful world these people live in."

I shook my head. "Assuming this is all true, what's with the animals?"

"Oh, I just brought them to see how they would handle the sleep." He shrugged. "Sorry about your goat, but I am a scientist, after all. And I had to bring you so that you wouldn't divulge my secret. Nobody knows about that cave, and much as I want to, well, I certainly don't want to play God with the future. I figured I could help some people, but if word got out, then there'd be chaos, with all the people that would want to sleep in that cave."

I stared at him. "You are crazy!"

"No he isn't!"

I turned towards the familiar voice. "Rory!" I ran to him and threw myself into his arms. "Rory, where have you been?" I stepped back to look at him. I was surprised to see his crutches were gone and he was standing on two legs. I gasped. "My God, you've got your leg back!"

"Well, sort of," he answered. He leaned over and lifted up his pant leg, revealing a flesh-coloured plastic limb. He put his pant leg down. "I can walk again."

I thought about what was happening. "So we are now in the future. That means that Uncle Sal..."

Mr. Wilfred shook his head. "Sorry, Mary, your uncle is long gone."

I bowed my head. "Poor Uncle Sal, he must've been beside himself when I went missing." My thoughts were interrupted by a deep rumble, followed by a screeching sound overhead. I screamed as a giant metal bird flew overhead.

Rory laughed. "Don't be afraid, Mary. That's just an example of what the Wright brothers started. Heck, you should see the horseless carriages they've got now!"

"Come folks, let's get these critters to a farm," Mr. Wilfred suggested. "We have a lot of exploring to do."

We headed out of the field. Rory turned to me. "Would you believe they've managed to put a man on the moon?" He smiled. "Oh, and there are no such things as Martians. At least, not at the moment..."

The Cougar and the Crow

Hattie stood in the middle of the farmer's field, chewing on a piece of straw. She shivered in the cool, autumn breeze as she scanned the barren field. The hay had been cut and collected, and there was a cold nip in the air. She sighed at the prospect of having to migrate once again. She was getting old and couldn't keep up with the younger crows any longer. The wind picked up, and she puffed her feathers out. If only she could find a way to stay home for the winter. But the bitter cold would kill her for sure...

Her thoughts were interrupted by a high-pitched shriek coming from the wooded area behind the farm. There's that dang cougar again, she thought to herself. Probably got herself another one of them rabbits. Hattie shook her head. What's a cougar doing around here, anyways? She should be crawling around in those mountains yonder... She heard another shriek, followed by several more. Hmmm... sounds like that cat's gotten herself into some trouble... Hattie flew off into the woods to investigate.

"Please leave me alone!" Jade shooed off the crows with her three good paws as she lay on her side, her broken leg curled up beneath her.

"What'sa matter, can't you catch a couple of measly crows?" one of them cackled.

The other crow joined in the laughter. "Not so tough now, are you, kitty cat?"

The two crows kept flying around the cougar, taking nips at her with their sharp beaks. Two more crows joined in. Jade was exhausted from trying to fight them off, and soon collapsed. She realized that she would die at the hands of these crows. She closed her eyes and waited.

"What is going on?" A loud voice echoed through the woods, causing the crows and the cougar to jump. They looked up into a tall oak tree and saw Hattie perched on a branch. "Get away from that poor beast! Can't you see she's injured?"

One of the crows waved his wing towards Jade. "Aw Hattie, it's just that miserable old wildcat who's been eating all the critters around here."

"Yeah," another crow said, "she deserves to die!"

Hattie looked at Jade, and saw the misery in her greenish gold cat's eyes. She knew she couldn't let this poor animal die at the hands of her kind. "No she doesn't. She's away from her home and is only trying to survive."

She flew down from the tree branch and stood next to the cougar's head. "She's injured. This isn't a fair fight."

"But Hattie..." a third crow moaned.

Hattie shook her head. "Look, we're the smartest birds in the world. Do you really want to waste all that intelligence on a dumb ol' cat?"

"Hey, who're you calling dumb?" Jade lifted her head and looked at Hattie, who only gave her a wink.

The crows all nodded. "You're right, Hattie." The fourth one said. "C'mon fellas, let's go find some blue jays to torment." The gang of crows flew off.

Jade breathed a sigh of relief. She smiled at Hattie. "Thank you so much ma'am. I thought I was going to die for sure!"

Hattie nodded. "And you would have." She hopped over to the cougar's hurt leg. "What happened to you?"

"I fell out of a tree."

Hattie looked surprised. "I thought cougars were good tree climbers."

"Yeah, so did I." Jade gave Hattie a grim smile. "Maybe you should've just let those crows kill me. I won't be able to hunt with this leg, and with winter just around the corner, that means I can't fatten up for hibernation." A tear escaped Jade's eye. "I'm doomed."

Hattie patted the cougar's head with her wing. "Don't cry, um... I'm Hattie; and you are?"

"Jade."

"Well Jade, what are you doing out here away from your mountains?"

Jade shrugged. "Some humans were making booming sounds with strange weapons. I think they were hunting for food. I got scared and ran into these woods to hide. I meant to go back, but there was lots of food here, so I stayed a while." She sighed. "Now I can't go back at all."

Hattie looked at Jade's leg. She brushed her wings lightly across the swollen area. "Well, at least it's a clean break. It just needs to heal." She took out her straw and began to chew on it. After a few moments, her face lit up. "I have a great idea! Let me fix your leg, and then we can get you back to your mountains."

"How are you going to do that?"

"You'll see! Don't go away!" Hattie flew off.

Jade smirked. "As if I can go anywhere with this leg..."

For the next few hours, Hattie flew back and forth, collecting straw, twigs and bits of mud and depositing them by Jade's broken leg. When her pile grew larger than she was, she began weaving the twigs with the straw while adding mud to hold it all together. When she completed a small piece, she put it on Jade's broken leg and continued to build the nest-like cast around her leg. By the end of the day, the cast was complete.

Hattie looked at her creation. "Not so bad, if I do say so myself. I guess all those years of making nests for my babies have paid off." She patted Jade on her backside. "Now, try not to move too much. This thing has to dry before you can walk on it. Get some sleep, and by tomorrow you should be fine."

Jade felt a wave of hope. "Thank you Hattie!" She closed her eyes and fell asleep.

Hattie looked at the young cougar and knew she couldn't leave her until she was safely back home in the mountains. She cuddled up to Jade's belly, fluffed up her feathers and settled into a deep sleep.

The next morning, Jade woke up, surprised to find the crow nearby nibbling on some dandelion leaves. "Why are you still here? I thought you would've gone home."

"You're not ready to be alone yet. Why, I'll bet you haven't eaten in a while." Hattie chuckled. "I could hear you belly grumbling all night! Rocked me to sleep, it did."

"I am rather hungry."

"What do cougars eat, besides rabbits? Maybe I can get you something."

"Well, we usually hunt for deer and mountain goats."

Hattie guffawed. "Okay, scrap that idea... Let me fly into town and see what I can find."

She flew off and returned a half an hour later with a large sack hanging from her claws.

"I managed to steal this from a human. She put it down while opening the door to one of those big vee-hickles they like to race around in." She turned the sack upside down and emptied the contents in front of Jade. The hungry cougar quickly attacked the food.

When she finished, she slowly got up on her broken leg and practiced walking on the cast, while Hattie tidied up the human garbage. "Hmm, I wonder what the golden arches on these containers mean?" she mumbled to herself.

Jade found the cast to be quite comfortable, and soon she headed towards the mountains. Hattie followed along, sometimes flying back and forth, and at other times perched on the cougar's back. The mountains would be several days of travel to reach, and slow going with Jade's broken leg. Hattie continued to fly into town to steal what human food she could, but soon the humans were onto her, and began to guard their sacks carefully, shooing her away.

By the time they reached the last leg of their journey, Jade was able to clumsily hunt small prey with Hattie's help, who would chase and shoo the critters in Jade's direction. Hattie noticed that the cougar was filling out quite nicely in time for her hibernation. She also noticed all the other crows were gathering together and taking off on their yearly trek south. She realized that she wouldn't be able to catch up to them, or to make that trek alone.

They reached the mountains on the tenth day of travel. Jade led them to her small cave, and there they collapsed in exhaustion. Jade was ready to go to sleep for the winter, so Hattie pecked the cast off her leg.

"The winter's sleep will heal that leg just fine," Hattie said.

Jade looked out of the cave. She could see the flocks of various birds flying southward. She looked at Hattie. "I guess you'll be heading for warmer climates now."

Hattie sighed and shook her head. "I'm too old. I don't think I can make that flight anymore." Her eyes filled with tears. "Yet I can't stay around here. I'll never be able to survive the cold winter."

"Oh yes you can. If all you need is warmth, you can stay here with me." Jade smiled at Hattie. "But you have to promise to go into town and steal human food occasionally. I really like that stuff with the golden arches!"

Hattie laughed. "It's a deal!" She extended her wing and Jade took it into her paw and shook it. Then Jade lay down and went to sleep. Hattie cuddled up to Jade's belly, fluffed up her feathers and also settled into a deep sleep.

The Unicorns and the Rain

Part I

The two unicorns sat on the hill, sated from grazing on the lush grass. The early morning brought a promise of another warm, sunny day. Below the hill, there was a bustle going on, entertaining the unicorns.

Aramis shook his head, tossing his lush mane to one side. "Look at this fine day. Do those fools really think the land will flood soon?"

"Rumour has it that it will rain for three fortnights straight," Lara said. "The human Noah and his sons have built that vessel to save humans and animals from drowning."

Aramis looked at the menagerie of animals lined up at the vessel. "They all seemed to believe it. Look at how willingly they wait to get on board."

"Yet all the humans laugh and scoff at Noah." Lara looked at Aramis. "What do you think, my love?"

"I think the humans are right. We are the only unicorns left. It is up to us to continue our species." Aramis nuzzled Lara's neck. "We are young yet and have plenty of time to do so. And it will not happen on an ark!"

Lara nodded. "Then we must keep from getting caught. They have been looking for us for days now. We must remain invisible."

"We have been blessed with magic. Time to use it." Aramis laid his head down and closed his eyes. Lara snuggled up beside him, and they slept in the morning sun, invisible to the rest of the world.

Several hours later, they awoke to a startling thunderbolt. They skies around them had gone dark with rain clouds.

Lara looked at Aramis with a worried expression. "It's just a thunderstorm, Lara." He consoled her. "Let's get to our cave."

They galloped further up the hill through the pouring rain and into their dry cave. From there, they watched as the relentless storm continued for hours. They could see the lowlands beginning to flood.

"Look, the humans are all running towards the mountains!" Lara said.

"Not to worry; the floods will never reach them. Or us." But Aramis sounded doubtful.

The rain continued for hours more. The hours turned into days, and then into weeks. The ark had been lifted by the floods and had disappeared beyond the horizon. The unicorns' hill was surrounded by water.

"If the rain doesn't stop soon, our cave will flood!" Lara panicked.

"Calm down, Lara, it can't continue much longer!"

But it did. A fortnight later, the water had reached the mouth of the cave. It began to trickle in.

Aramis sighed. "Oh Lara, perhaps Noah was right. We should've gone to the ark when he called us."

Tears fell from Lara's face. "We are doomed. And so is our species. No amount of magic can help us now."

The water was quickly flooding the cave. Aramis and Lara left it and climbed to the very top of the hill. They could see the mountains, or what was left of them, poking out from the endless sea. They were crowded with humans.

"Aramis, this is the end."

"Yes, my love, it is."

And together they lay on the hilltop, hooves locked, until the waves swept them away.

Part II

The Angel Gabriel sat on the puffy white cloud, next to Aramis and Lara. "The Almighty One is disappointed in both of you," he told them. "He asked Noah to save the animals. And what did you do? You laughed at Noah, like the humans did. Now there are no more unicorns left on earth."

Aramis hung his head. "I know. The Almighty One gave us magic, and we refused to believe that anything could happen to us. Or at least I did." He looked at Lara. "You trusted me, and now you're here."

Lara smiled. "I wouldn't want to be anywhere else."

They watched the earth from the cloud. The waters had receded, and the ark was able to land on a mountaintop. Noah's family and the animals slowly worked their way down the mountain as the water level lowered.

The Angel Gabriel sighed. "Ah well, what is done is done. The Almighty One has decided to forgo giving magic to animals. From now on, they will rely on instinct." He smiled at the sad unicorns. "Do not feel bad, my friends. He is very forgiving, and will be happy to have you among his Heavenly Animal Kingdom!"

They continued to watch as the earth sprouted new growth under the warm, sunny day. There was an electric feel to the air, as though the world had been born anew, after the rain.

Party Time

The pressure was building in the large passageway, as millions of families crowded around the entrance. Parents were fussing around their children, giving last minute instructions and wishing them luck. The children themselves were excited to be embarking on a new adventure. They had never been outside the passageway, had never seen the light of day. The parents could only hope that it was daylight; it was much more exciting, and the chances of survival for the next generation of cold viruses were much higher if their hosts were among other humans.

As the children made their way to the front, several loud booms could be heard. Shouts of "Hurry children, the sneeze is about to go off! Good bye!" could be heard from the parents. They stood back as the final boom approached, and the wind shot through the passageway, taking the children out through the entrance.

Gren was holding several of his older sister's hands. Vica was instructed to stay close to Gren at all times; he was a lazy virus, her parents told her, and needed direction. She wondered how hard it could possibly be to find a new host. Wouldn't the sneeze simply attach the young viruses to another human?

She soon understood the complications, as the searing bright light blinded her for a moment. But then she was able to see, and the beauty of what her parents described as "colour" took her breath away. Not that she had breath, she chided herself. But she had colour, as did all the other viruses. Beautiful little pink, blue and green swirls of

216

colour, with hundreds of little hands ready to grasp their new homes.

As they slowly flew into space, Gren yelled out, "Party time!"

Vica looked at her brother. "What are you talking about?"

"It's party time, Sis," he chuckled. "Look at this place. No parents, millions of kids! Time to par-tay!"

Vica sighed. "For heaven's sake, Gren, we're supposed to find a new host if we want to survive. We don't have time to party!"

"We have a couple of hours," he retorted. "That's plenty of time for a virus. Look we're still floating!"

Vica looked around her. Her parents described what a human would look like, but she couldn't see anything like it. She felt herself beginning to fall. "Look Gren, we're descending! I think we may end up on an inanimate object. That's not good!"

And indeed, the group of travelling viruses all landed on a large, flat surface.

Gren shrugged. "Oh well, we still have a chance for survival if we can get picked up by a human hand. But for now... It's party time!" He let go of Vica's hands and floated off to see find his friends.

"Gren!" she shouted after him. "I'm not supposed to let you out of my sight!" She floated after him.

When she caught up, he grinned at her wickedly and said, "Pull my finger!"

"You have thousands of fingers! What are you talking about?"

"I don't know. I heard it's something humans do, and apparently it gets a few laughs."

Vica rolled her eyes. "Never mind the laughs. We need to find a host."

"Well, we can't travel outside our viral area, so the host will just have to find us. In the mean time...."

"I know, I know... party time." She stayed close to him as he sought out his friends.

For the next while, Gren and Vica wandered around, greeting friends they came across. It was indeed a party atmosphere, with the kids enjoying their first taste of freedom. Together they enjoyed the new sights and poked friendly fun at each other's unusual colours. Several groups gathered together and, holding hands, danced around in circles. Vica had found her own friends and began to relax and enjoy the party.

After a while, Vica found herself getting tired and sat down. She looked around and noticed the other viruses had settled down a bit. The dancing had stopped, as did the steady buzz of conversation. She suddenly realized that a fair bit of time had gone by and no host had made itself available yet. The viruses were beginning to die.

She got up to look for Gren. As she floated through the crowds, she noticed an eerie calmness. Everybody was resting and trying to keep their strength up. Finally, she saw Gren and joined him.

"Vica, I'm scared," he said.

"Me too," she replied and they grasped several hands and sat down together.

Suddenly somebody yelled, "Look!" Everyone looked up and saw some movement overhead.

"Hands!" Gren shouted. "They're human hands!" Everybody cheered. "It's party time!" he shouted.

"Not yet, Gren! We still have to come in contact with one of those hands." Vica reminded him. "We're not out of the woods yet!"

"Have a little faith, Sis!" Gren looked puzzled. "Um, what are woods?"

"I don't know," Vica said. "It's just another human saying." She looked up. The hands kept wavering over the crowd of viruses, but they were getting nowhere near. She sighed. "Even if we do attach ourselves to those hands, we still have to wait for them to transfer us to the nasal passageways. We don't have much time left."

She felt weak and leaned back, still holding hands with Gren. "I don't think we're going to make it..."

Suddenly, it became dark and she felt a heaviness surrounding her. This is it, she thought, we're goners. But then the light returned and she felt herself being sucked through the air. She looked down and noticed two human hands on the surface, then looked back and saw a human face looming over the group of viruses. Then everything was once again black, but very familiar and comfortable.

She was regaining her strength. Somebody yelled out, "We're in the nasal passageway!" and everybody cheered. She still felt Gren's hands in her own.

"The human must've laid his head down directly onto the surface with its face right on top of us." Gren laughed. "We have a host!"

"So we do!" With a sigh of relief, Vica let go of his hands. "Now what, little brother?"

Gren let out a hoot. "It's party time!"

The Lion and the Mermaid

Fuoco felt the familiar terror as he flailed his paws uselessly in the water. His head submerged and then resurfaced, but not before he swallowed a mouthful of saltwater. He gasped for air, only to take in another mouthful of water. He submerged once again, and tried to fight the urge to succumb to the power of the water...

"Fuoco!" He could hear the sea calling his name. Hands reached out to shake his body. No, not hands; paws. He woke up with a start.

Maxi, his young friend, was leaning over him. "You're having that nightmare again, Fuoco."

Fuoco groaned. "Yes I am, and I wish you wouldn't wake me up before..." He sighed.

Maxi nodded. "It's that sea creature, isn't it? You wish to see her in your dreams, don't you?" When Fuoco remained silent, he continued. "She saved your life. I understand your gratitude, but you seem to be obsessed. You haven't been yourself lately."

"My friend, you don't know half the truth." Fuoco got up and signalled for Maxi to follow him. Together, they moved away from the rest of the pride, until they were far enough away to speak without disturbing the other sleeping lions.

They stopped and turn towards each other. Maxi couldn't help admiring the full mane his friend had acquired over the years. His eyes still had the intense look of the fine king that he was. He felt sad knowing that his days on the throne were numbered.

As if reading his mind, Fuoco said, "Maxi, I'm not getting any younger. Breeding season is coming up, and I am aware that the pride will be looking for a new king."

Maxi looked away.

Fuoco continued. "Oh, don't be ashamed, my friend. It's all part of our breed's survival. You will be among the younger males who will fight me for my throne. I will either bravely fight until death, or I will simply leave the pride." He sighed. "Before I fell into the water, there was no question that I would fight for my title as king. After all, there is nothing for me outside my pride. But now that I have seen the sea creature, I feel as if I still have something to live for."

Maxi stared at him. "With all due respect, Fuoco, have you lost your mind? You are terrified of the water! How would you even be able to find her?"

"I don't know." Fuoco hung his head. "I just know that I must find her." He felt Maxi's warm paw on his arm.

"You are still mourning Liza, aren't you?" Maxi looked away. "I don't mean to shame you, but there is a rumour among the lions that you purposely jumped into the water in order to join her."

"I know, Maxi. Liza drowned in the same waters that I almost did. And a year later, almost to the date, at that. Quite the coincidence, don't you think?" Fuoco looked into Maxi's eyes. "Ah Maxi, I do miss her. If I left the pride, she would have come with me. And I would have been able to leave with dignity. But I didn't jump into the water to kill myself. She wouldn't have wanted that. No, I was just standing on the edge of the rocks thinking about her when I lost my footing and simply fell in."

Maxi nodded. "I believe you. And I am grateful that you were saved by that sea creature. But-"

"I know, I know, I shouldn't be obsessed with her." Fuoco chuckled. "Just humour me, will you. Humour this old man and let him have his fun while he can."

"Fuoco, you're not that old! You still have plenty of fire left in you! Your mother named you well."

"Yes, she did. Now let's get back to the pride."

Maxi laughed. "Of course. An old lion like you needs his beauty rest."

"Old lion, huh!" Fuoco playfully tackled Maxi, and after a few moments of wrestling, the two friends returned to the pride.

When Maxi woke up the next morning, Fuoco was gone.

* * * *

Fuoco walked along the beach towards the rocks. He was exhausted from lack of sleep and from his trek across the plains. He fought back his fear at the sight of the water and the taste of salt on his tongue. When he finally reached the rocks, he decided to rest before attempting to climb them. Fear is best conquered on a good night's sleep, he thought, even if the sun was coming up.

He woke up extremely thirsty, with the sun beating down on him. He made his way to the shallow tributary on the other side of the rocks, where fresh, cool water flowed into the sea. He padded into the water, drank deeply, and submerged himself, carefully keeping his head above water. He climbed out and shook himself dry.

He went back to the base of the rocks and ignoring his fear, proceeded to climb them. They were not very high off the sand, and getting to the top was simple. It was the climb outwards as the rocks jutted out into the sea that made Fuoco uneasy. He stood on the first rock and looked out at the water. The sea was gentler today than it was the day he fell in. The rocks looked dry. Still, he decided he wouldn't go right to the edge.

As he made his way to the edge, he was startled as something jumped out of the water and onto the furthest rock. The figure looked familiar and he blinked as he realized that it was the sea creature that had saved him. She sat up on the rock with her back to him, and didn't notice him. He took a moment to study her.

She was half human, with a long, dark, silky mane, or, as Fuoco tried to remember his knowledge of human creatures, it would be called "hair". The sun picked up shimmering silver streaks when she shook her head. She turned sideways, and he noticed that she was completely hairless, except for the dark streaks of hair just above her eyes, and the fluttery hairs along her eyelids. Her torso was somewhat thin, if he was to compare her to the humans he's seen travelling through his homeland. He found himself staring at her teats; no, breasts. They were quite fascinating, although he wasn't sure why.

He tore his eyes away from her breasts to study the lower half of her body. She didn't have legs, as humans were apt to do, but rather a fish tail. It was a rich teal colour, with a large, translucent fin. Upon closer inspection, he realized that it didn't have scales like a fish, but it was smooth, similar to the texture of her skin.

Just then she turned towards him and their eyes met. She started for a moment, not expecting him to be there, and then her eyes widened in recognition. Her face broke into a bright smile, revealing sparkling white teeth. Fuoco noticed the slight wrinkling around her eyes as the smile reached them. He caught the twinkle in her dark eyes and felt a tightening in his chest.

"Well, hello!" she called out to him.

"Uh, h-hello," he stuttered as he continued to stare into her eyes.

"Could you come a little closer? It's a bit harder for me to move across these rocks."

Fuoco tore his eyes away from hers so that he could concentrate. He tried to ignore the now rougher waves as he slowly picked his way across the uneven surfaces of the various rocks, which had been piled together by the sea at its angrier moments. When he reached the last large, flat rock where the sea creature was perched, he let out an audible sigh of relief.

The sea creature chuckled. "You need not fear the water while I'm here. You know you are safe with me."

"I know I am," Fuoco nodded. "Ah, I didn't have a chance to thank you for saving my life."

"You're welcome." She smiled as Fuoco continued to stare at her. "I'm a mermaid, in case you're wondering."

"Oh, of course. I couldn't remember the term used describe, um..."

"Half human, half fish." The mermaid laughed. "My name is Teale." She held up her teal-coloured tail. "For obvious reasons."

"And I'm Fuoco. That's an Italian word... oh, but you probably wouldn't know about countries and such."

"Of course I do," Teale said. "We fish do travel in schools, you know."

Fuoco laughed. "That was a terrible joke."

Teale laughed as well. "I've swam the Mediterranean Sea. I know Fuoco means "fire". I've never seen fire, but I know it doesn't do well in water."

She bent her tail up and wrapped her arms around them, as humans were apt to do with their legs. He was disappointed that her breasts were now covered. She patted a spot on the rock next to her, and he sat down.

"Why do you come out here all the time?" Teale asked.

He looked at her. "You know I come here often?"

"Yes." She nodded towards the sea. "This is a pretty area. I swim out here all the time. The sea can get a bit rough, so there isn't a lot of sea life venturing here, but I can handle it better than most fish. And I can see the shore from beneath the surface."

Fuoco sighed. "What a shame you weren't here when my Liza fell in and drowned."

Teale's eyes widened. "I heard about a lion drowning around here about a year ago!"

"That was Liza, my mate. She was out here with a few lionesses, exploring the area. They all walked along the shore, but my Liza was a bold one. She went in further." He looked out towards the sea. "A wave caught her and swept her in."

He felt her hand, surprisingly warm, on the side of his face. He turned towards her and their eyes met. "I wish I was here that day too. Perhaps I could have saved her and spared you the pain that so obviously shows in your eyes." She smiled sadly, and Fuoco tried to return the smile.

"I never could master the art of smiling," he told her. The mood lightened as she giggled.

They spent the morning in the warm sun. Teale would jump into the water periodically to keep from dehydrating while Fuoco climbed down the rocks to the fresh water. Climbing became easier for him, most likely because of Teale's presence. He wondered why he wasn't more embarrassed about depending on her for his safety. He was, after all, king of his pride. He was a protector, not a protected. But he was also smart enough to realize that this was Teale's territory, and not his.

They talked about themselves. He told her about his many children with Liza, and she told him of her son and daughter, now both grown merman and mermaid. He felt oddly jealous when she spoke of her husband, a term he understood meant "mate", but then chided himself. They were two totally different creatures. Even if she was available, she would still be somewhat unavailable. However, she did have a wonderful sense of humour and he found himself laughing at her stories and anecdotes.

Soon the sun was overhead, and they both felt hungry. "Leave it to me," Teale said, and she jumped into the water. "I hope you like fish!" Without waiting for an answer, she dove underwater and disappeared. A few minutes later, she resurfaced and threw a large fish onto the rocks, where it flapped helplessly. Teale did this several times, until six fish were flapping around on the rocks.

She jumped back up onto the edge of the rock. Fuoco watched as she erotically balanced on her hands and what would be her hip area if she was human. Her gleaming wet breasts were half covered by stands of silky wet hair, and he found himself getting excited. Nonsense, he thought, she's a sea creature. He tore his eyes away and concentrated on the now motionless fish.

"Dig in, and be careful of the bones!" Teale picked up a fish and unceremoniously bit into it. Fuoco suppressed a chuckle as this tiny creature, noisily chomped through her lunch. So much like his Liza, he thought, and then chided himself for comparing the two very different females. He bent down, picked up a fish and joined in the noisy feast.

When they were done, Teale swept the fish bones into the water and yawned. This caused Fuoco to yawn and they both laughed. Teale pointed to a shady area beneath the rocks, where the waves gently lapped against the shore. Fuoco nodded, and climbed down the rocks to the dry area. Teale wiggled across the wet sand to meet him. He lay down and Teale curled up against him, making sure her tail stayed in the shallow water. Together, they fell asleep.

* * * *

Fuoco felt a pair of hands shaking him. No, it was paws. No, hands! He woke up with a start. Teale was still lying next to him, but she was staring at him through panicked eyes. She looked deathly pale. He noticed that she was no longer submerged in water. In fact, the tide had gone out.

It was when she pushed herself up onto her hands and knees, and then up into a standing position, that he realized her tail was gone and in its place were human legs.

She took a few deep breaths and shook her wobbly legs out one at a time. She caught Fuoco's intense stare and smiled at him sheepishly. The colour seemed to have returned to her face. Fuoco realized his jaw was hanging. He closed it.

"Surprise," Teale chuckled weakly.

"Well," was all Fuoco could say. He tried not to stare at the soft patch of hair between her legs.

"Um, this happens to mermaids when they are out of the water for a long period of time."

"I see."

Teale blushed as Fuoco studied her intensely from head to toe. "You are very beautiful," he finally said.

"Oh, uh," she stuttered. "Thank you." She looked away from him, and turned her head up towards the sky. "Oh no, it's getting late!"

Fuoco then noticed that the sun was low.

"I have to go!" Teale said. "My husband will wonder where I am!" She turned towards the water.

"No, please stay!" Fuoco called out to her, as she waded in.

"I can't!" She dived into the water. She surfaced and dived again. Her tail was back. She resurfaced and yelled, "I'll be back tomorrow, I promise!" She dived back in and disappeared.

Fuoco stood in the warm sand and stared out at the water for a long time. He thought about the last few hours he had just spent with the lovely mermaid. He recalled some of her jokes and giggled. He then giggled at the fact that she could make a grown lion giggle. He thought about her human form, and sighed. He realized that he wanted her. Except for Liza, he had never felt this way about any female, lioness or otherwise.

He lay back down beneath the rocks, where only minutes ago, she had lain with him. He was hungry, but he decided not to hunt. He would wait here for her. She had promised to come back tomorrow. He closed his eyes and dreamed about fearlessly swimming in the sea with a lovely sea creature at his side.

* * * *

He felt something tugging at his mane, and opened his eyes. She was leaning over him, a dreamy look in her eyes, hands entangled in his fur. She stared deep into his eyes, and he felt a wave of intense heat wash over him. She let go of him. He got up on his hands and knees, then pushed himself up onto his legs. His legs? He gasped as he realized he had taken on a human form. He stared at his hands as he moved them front to back, then looked down at his naked body.

He heard her giggle, and looked up. She was smiling as she moved toward him. He looked into her eyes once again, and knew that she somehow transformed him. She was also in human form.

They stood close to each other, and then found themselves wrapped in each other's arms. They stared into each other's eyes, drinking in the lust. Then their lips met. He gently tasted her soft mouth, rubbing his tongue across her lips. She parted them slightly, allowing his tongue to rub across her the top of her teeth. He felt her shudder, and she opened her mouth, allowing him to taste more.

As their tongues made love, their hands explored. Feathery touches travelled down their backs, hands tightening across buttocks. Back up and around, his travelled down to her breasts, where his fingers lightly caressed her nipples. She pulled back to gasp, and he quickly covered her mouth again, still hungry for her taste. He could feel her hands travel down, and it was his turn to gasp, breaking their kiss as her small hand wrapped around his manhood and gently squeezed.

He kissed her lightly, and carried his kisses down her chin and her neck. She tilted her head back, and he nibbled her neck. She moaned. He ran his tongue down her chest until he reached a nipple. There, he began to lick the taut bud, while his hand played with the other nipple, gently squeezing and releasing. She moaned again, and thrust her pelvis to his.

He released her breasts, picked her up, and laid her down on the warm, sandy beach by the water. The waves lapped gently against her as he bent over her to continue feasting on her breasts. He held both in his hands, and took turns licking each nipple. Her hands were entangled in his hair as she arched her back towards him.

"Oh please," she moaned.

"Not yet," he answered in a husky voice.

His mouth locked onto a nipple, and he sucked, causing her to moan loudly. He released the luscious rosebud, and his tongue continued down her stomach. He reached her soft patch of hair and stopped for a moment to look up at her. He could see that she was anxiously awaiting him. He buried his face between her legs and proceeded to lick her feminine folds.

Slowly, he worked his tongue around her tiny swelling. He felt her hands gripping his hair even tighter as he brought his tongue into her sweet juices. His tongue flicked in and out, in and out, until she arched her back and called out his name in ecstasy. He held her hips tight as he continued to take in her sweetness, until she once again reached climax.

"Now, please now!"

"Yes, my love, now!"

He brought himself up and over her. Their lips met and locked into a passionate kiss as he entered her. She moaned beneath his mouth as he slowly moved inside her. Their hands locked and he brought them up beside her head, all the while still kissing. His movement picked up speed, and she brought her legs up, locking them around his waist. Their momentum picked up and their kiss broke as they both became breathless. Once again, she called out his name. He joined her, and together they rode the ultimate wave of passion.

They came down from the wave together and kissed once more. He then pulled away and looked into her eyes, where he saw passion and, could it be possible, love? He shifted his weight off of her and lay down beside her. He noticed the water had climbed up and around them, the waves caressing them both. He pulled her further up onto the shore, and then wrapped his arms and legs around her. She looked at him and smiled, and then snuggled her face into his chest. They fell asleep.

When Fuoco woke up, he was once again a lion. Teale was lying next to him, fish tail resting in the shallow water. He nuzzled her face, and she woke up with a start. She slowly pulled herself up to a sitting position. She looked into his eyes, and he noticed that she looked pale and tired. She turned away from his gaze.

"We must never do this again," she told him.

"But why?" Fuoco asked. "It was the most beautiful thing I've ever experienced!"

Teale smiled sadly. "Yes, it was beautiful. But there are many reasons why we cannot continue this."

"But I love you!" Fuoco blurted out without thinking. He didn't have to think. The words came from his heart.

"Oh Fuoco, I love you too," Teale sighed. "But that isn't enough. First of all, I'm limited with my powers. Turning into a complete human is hard on me, but transferring that power to you drained me. It can eventually kill me. And besides, "she sighed again. "I belong to my husband."

"Well, he must not love you enough if you need to seek love in the arms of another!"

"Oh, it isn't his fault! He loves me dearly. It's just that sometimes... I don't know. There just seems to be something missing." Teale looked at him. "And whatever it is that's missing, I seemed to have found it in you."

Fuoco nodded. "Perhaps I do understand. You have filled a void in me as well, what with my Liza gone."

Teale smiled. "Well, Fuoco, at least now I understand what fire is. You certainly brought it into my life."

"And you taught me that love doesn't have to be limited to one person." Fuoco lowered his head onto his paws. "But now what do we do?"

"I don't know. I love my husband, but I'm in love with you. You love me, but you're in love with Liza." Teale nodded. "I think I need to go back home for a while and think about this."

"Home?" Fuoco looked perplexed. "But I don't..." He was silent for a moment, and then nodded too. "Yes, I do believe I must go back home too."

Teale pulled herself into the water. "Then I will look for you in a few days." She waved. "Good bye, my love! I will see you soon!" And she dove into the waves.

Fuoco stared out at the sea. "I certainly hope so, my Angelfish. I certainly hope so." And he headed back to the plains.

* * * *

Maxi watched the familiar figure slowly work across the plains towards him. He glanced around at the other lions, but they were all sound asleep after feasting on some fresh kill. Although in Fuoco's absence they have not fought for a new king yet, Maxi was regarded as the strongest lion, and the pride understood that he would watch over them. Perhaps no one would fight him and he would be declared king anyway.

But now, as Fuoco came nearer, Maxi realized, and regretted, that there may be bloodshed after all. He quietly got up to greet his old friend.

"You look well, Fuoco," Maxi said. "Perhaps sea life becomes you?"

Fuoco chuckled. "Let's just say I'm still a little wet behind the ears where sea life is concerned."

Maxi chuckled along with him. Then he looked serious. "Happy as I am to see you, my friend, you do realize that this complicates things."

Fuoco looked at the sleeping pride and nodded. "Yes, it does. At first, I was happy to just leave and never come back. But Maxi, I have found my sea creature! She has helped me understand many things about myself. I know that I can love again. Liza's love made me strong, but then her death weakened me. And now Teale's love has brought my strength back to me."

Maxi nodded. "Ah yes, what is it the humans say? Behind every strong man there is a strong woman."

"Humans can be quite smart," Fuoco said.

"Not to mention tasty!" Both lions chuckled.

Maxi said, "So now you've come back to fight me because you found love. That is odd. Why did you not stay with this Teale?"

Fuoco shrugged. "She belongs to another."

"And so you wish me to kill you?"

"What makes you think I won't kill you?"

Maxi remained silent. He looked back at the still sleeping lions. "Fuoco, nobody has seen you yet. You can still leave here without getting hurt."

Fuoco shook his head. "I'm sorry Maxi, but this is something I must do.

Maxi sighed. "I understand." He nodded towards the recent kill. "There is still meat left. Eat and sleep; get your strength up. Then we will fight."

Maxi placed a paw on Fuoco's arm and then went back to the pride.

* * * *

After his meal, Fuoco laid down to rest. He knew that he might never see Teale again.

Maxi was very strong and would surely kill him. But he also knew that he could never live with himself, or with Teale, if he didn't fight like the mighty king that he was.

With Teale on his mind, he fell into a deep sleep.

A mighty roar awakened him. He saw Maxi standing in front of his now awake pride of lions. Fuoco shook himself awake and went over to stand in front of him. They bowed to each other. The challenge was understood. They began to fight.

The other lions stood back as Maxi and Fuoco circled each other. Then they jumped at each other at the same time, colliding in midair and crashing to the ground together. For the next several minutes, they wrestled fiercely, each trying to sink his teeth into the throat of the other while keeping his own throat clear of the danger.

Both lions fought bravely, but after a few minutes, Fuoco found himself getting tired. He knew he was no match for the much younger Maxi, but his pride kept him from giving in too soon. Maxi was delivering many bites and scratches, and soon Fuoco succumbed to his wounds and collapsed. Through the painful haze, he could see Maxi standing over him. He closed his eyes and waited for the final blow.

He was surprised when he felt Maxi's powerful jaw close around his throat, but not sink into his skin. Maxi's jaw stayed there for a few moments, and then Fuoco felt him pull away. "He is dead!" came the sound of his friend's voice. "Come now, my pride, we must leave our old king alone to die with dignity."

Fuoco lay there for a few minutes, contemplating what had just happened. Maxi had allowed him to live. His friend gave him the chance to leave his throne with his head held high, so to speak. The lions would think Fuoco died the same way he lived, as a mighty king.

He slowly opened his eyes. He could see the lions wandering further away from the area. Soon, he could no longer see them. He slowly got up, wincing at the pain throughout his battered body. He limped in the opposite direction of where the lions had gone, and slowly made his way back to the sea.

* * * *

Teale swam towards the shore. She hoped that Fuoco would be there, waiting for her. If not, she would wait for him. Not that she had any news for him. She was unable to make a decision as to whether she would continue to see him or not. She knew she should end their relationship and go back to her family, but Fuoco was much a part of her now. He held a piece of her heart in his paws, and there was nothing she could do about it now. She was hopelessly in love with him.

She reached the rocks and jumped up onto her usual perch. She was shocked to see Fuoco lying there. He was covered in cuts and scratches.

"Fuoco, my love!" She cried out. She wiggled over the rocks to where he was lying. She was relieved to see that he was breathing.

He opened his eyes. "Teale," he whispered.

Teale threw her arms around his neck. ""What happened?"

"I fought for my throne, but I lost." He coughed.

"I see," Teale said. "Well, perhaps you lost your throne, but I imagine you won the fight."

Fuoco nodded. "I think you're right. Although I don't know for how long I'll be able to keep that title."

"Oh my darling, how long have you been here?"

"A couple of days, I think." Fuoco coughed again.

"Wait," Teale said, and she disappeared into the water.

"Don't worry, I' won't be going anywhere," Fuoco whispered. He fell asleep.

The feel of cold water on his face awakened him. He opened his eyes and saw Teale leaning over him with a shell in her hand. "I have fresh water from the stream. Drink." She held the shell to his mouth and he drank.

When he was done, he looked at Teale gratefully. "How did you manage..." But then he noticed her human legs. "You changed your form."

Teale smiled. "How else can I take care of you?"

"Oh my Angelfish, I'm so ill."

Teale brushed a tear from her face. "Yes, I know." She lay down beside him.

"You look pale. I don't want you to get weak," he told her.

"Don't you worry about me," she said. "Just get yourself better."

"That's what I'm trying to do." He fell asleep.

* * * *

"Fuoco! Fuoco!"

He opened his eyes. "What?"

"Fuoco, come to me."

He looked towards the voice. He saw Liza floating over the water. "It's time, Fuoco. Time to join me."

Fuoco got up. The pain was gone, and he felt much lighter and happier than he had for a long time. He floated towards Liza. "Yes, it's time." He reached out and took Liza's paw. Then he turned around and looked back at his body. Teale was leaning over him, crying heavily.

"Do not worry about her," Liza said. "She will be fine. She has her mate. Just as I now have mine."

"I loved her," Fuoco said. He held out his other paw. In it, he held a small flame. "I'm afraid I took a piece of her heart with me."

Liza nodded. "Yes, I know. And she loved you. I was happy to see you found love again." She tugged at Fuoco's paw. "But now we must go." Fuoco took the flame and pressed it into his heart. And together with Liza, he floated over the water and up into the fluffy white clouds above.

* * * *

Teale didn't know how long she laid there with Fuoco. She felt weak from dehydration and from the pain in her heart. She knew she had to get into the water, although all she wanted to do was lay there and die with him.

"But you're with Liza now, aren't you?" she whispered. "And so you should be." She kissed him on his face. "I must go now. I can only hope you know how much I love you."

She got up and jumped into the water. She felt her strength return, but she also felt a large void in her heart. She placed her hand over her chest to ease the pain there. When she pulled it away, she was surprised to see a bright flame floating gently on her hand.

She smiled. She knew it was fire. And she knew it was a piece of Fuoco's heart. She pressed the flame back into her chest and dove down into the sea.

Dedicated to Clay 1958 – 2008